Billy Baggins and the Bobbits

I0517451

For Lainey, Tom, Eddie and Melody

Billy Baggins and Curtis Hennig

The greatest adventure story ever told begins within the walls of number 36 Wess ngton Avenue. But which 36? For there are two on this street. One genuine and one an imposter, because - *with the top screw missing on the steel number 9 that sits to the right of the number 3* - the 9 on the door of 39 Wessington Avenue is permanently flipped upside down. So, it is probably truer to say that our story begins at the 36 Wessington Avenue that is in fact number 39, the home of Billy Baggins. The real number 36 may have been a better place to start because Billy, as often was the case, found himself in a spot of bother.

"Why can't you be more like Curtis?" Billy's Mum bellowed from the bottom of the stairs. "His room is always tidy. His Mum told me that he washes and irons his own clothes and then he folds them using origami techniques. He makes crowns from his t-shirts and swans from his pants - he uses them as decorations to make his bedroom look nice! And Curtis' shoes are always immaculate. They certainly aren't always covered in muck, like yours. Have you seen the state of the kitchen floor? I don't ask for much. I would just like you to try and keep the place clean, like Curtis does."

Curtis Hennig. Otherwise known as Mr Perfect, the golden boy who could do no wrong.

Comparisons to Curtis were something Billy did not welcome. After all, who could compare? Curtis had read every work by Shakespeare by the time he was five, he was the world record holder in nine different athletic events for his age group and he could play several instruments fluently. Heck, Curtis even performed mouth to mouth resuscitation on a man who had a heart attack and collapsed in the middle of street last year and brought him back to life! It was bad enough that he lived across the road, but Billy had to put up with him in school too. He was even sat next to him in class. It was torture! After every single question that Mr Higgins asked, Curtis' hand would be proudly raised, his armpit lodged tightly against Billy's face. But *so* amazing was Curtis Hennig that he never even smelt of B.O, even in the middle of summer. His armpit always smelled like a forest of pine trees after a heavy shower of springtime rain.

Billy sat in his messy room and thought about how he would be glad to see the back of his nemesis. You see, Curtis was starting boarding school in September, moving nearly one hundred miles away to lodge at St Barty's; the school for the filthy rich, ridiculously posh, and incredibly talented. Curtis was not particularly rich, he was a bit snooty - but not overly posh, but he was definitely talented, so he had been awarded a place at the prestigious school. Now this was no easy feat. Apparently only one child wins a scholarship to the school each year. To be selected you need to be an absolute genius, and in more than one field. But Curtis was fantastic in *all* that he did!

Of course, Billy only knew all this as he would regularly read Curtis' post. You see Curtis lived at the real number 36 Wessington Avenue and while any postman worth his salt would manage to deliver the appropriate letters in the appropriate door, the local postie was at least one hundred years old, with glasses so thick that it was as if he had two goldfish bowls attached to his face. So, it was no real surprise that the post was always a pic and mix of jumbled up letters. And Billy often found the invitation of opening Curtis' mail, which frequently arrived through his letter box, a temptation too great to resist.

Billy looked out the window and scanned the neighbourhood for signs of life. Across the street he could see a slither of Curtis' garden and of course, Curtis was outside! There he sat, crossed legged, gentling caressing the strings of his lute, a flop of golden locks cascading down his chiselled face like a waterfall of golden yarn. At the bottom of the garden was a target of shrinking coloured rings – black - blue –

red - with three arrows firmly lodged in the small yellow bullseye. Billy never could understand why Curtis bothered practicing h s archery skills anymore. Why practice when you have already reached perfection?

Yes, Billy would be very-glad indeed to see the back of Mr Perfect.

Suddenly Billy woke from his Curtis daydream and realised his Mum was still ranting.

"And do you know that Curtis studies architecture in his spare time? That new conservatory on the side of their house - he designed it! Apparently, Cynthia goes in there every evening and Curtis whips her up some dinner. Last night he made her beef wellington with potato fondants, carrot puree and a red wine jus. I am not asking you to build an extension or cook me a fancy dinner, although it would be nice, I just want your room tidy. And I want it sorted by tonight!"

Gazing around his room made B lly's mood sink ever deeper. There were clothes scattered everywhere.

Cups and saucers, with food that bore no resemblance to what it once was, were piled high in the corner and thousands of Lego bricks were scattered across the floor - a painful trap for unsuspecting bare feet! Billy knew he best get started. It was only just gone four, but the state of the place meant that he would need every remaining second of the day to sort out this catastrophe. But before he began, Billy paced over to the window and shut it tightly to drown out the noise of Curtis, who had begun whistling bird calls, while flocks of pigeons, robins and finches flapped around him, landing on his outstretched arms like he was the Messiah. Billy shook his head as he turned away from the window. He must tidy his room!

The Midnight Visitors

"Ouch! Comrades, please help me - I fear I have stepped on a cursed dagger. I have never experienced such pain. I do not believe that my foot can be saved. One of you will have to cut it off from my ankle. Be swift, dear friends."

"Don't be daft, you fool! That is no dagger. It a just a small plastic cuboid - nothing more than a child's construction toy. Now, please focus on the mission.........Oh my, look. There he is. I cannot believe we finally get to meet him."

"Friends, whilst this is indeed a joyous occasion, there is something deeply troubling that I must bring to your attention. A large furry snake has just slithered onto my foot, and I believe it to be highly poisonous. I am very scared, and I think I may require...my Mummy!"

"You need to calm down. You are as nervous as a Tilly Tally at the feast of Hortigar! That 'snake' is nothing more than a sock. It is what humans use to contain the stench of their feet. Now if you don't be quiet, you shall wake him."

"But we need to wake him, don't we? How else are we to talk with him?"

"Well…. yes, I suppose we do need to wake him. Right then, give him a bit of a shake."

Wearily, Billy peeled open his sticky eyelids. What time was it? It felt like the middle of the night, but then why was the room so bright? Billy rubbed his still sleepy eyes to stir them into life. And then, what he saw before him, startled him to the core.

At the foot of his bed, illuminated by an eerie turquoise glow, stood three short and stout creatures. While they appeared humanlike in many ways, the tips of their ears were pointed and their noses upturned, like a sounder of prim and proper pigs. Their bodies, which were somewhat covered by plain hessian sack cloth tunics, seemed to be covered entirely by a coarse fur. And from the bottom of their tunics protruded long, slender tails.

Billy shot up in bed like a rocket. "Who are you? And what are you doing in my room?"

One of the creatures smiled at him, baring a crooked row of large yellowish-brown teeth. "Fear not, we mean you no harm."

"We have been waiting our whole lives to meet you," spoke another.

"I cannot believe we are finally here," said the third creature, bobbing up and down like a young boy needing a wee.

The three creatures then just stood there for a while looking at Billy, grinning like star struck teenagers stood before their favourite popstar. Finally, one of them piped up, "Allow me to introduce myself, I am Gringo, chief scout and finder of the bobbit people. This is Ravenbeard, and the bobbit to my right is Frodo Fatlips.

The bobbits waved coyly to Billy.

It was such a strange thing that was happening, and perhaps it was a situation that he should have taken more seriously, but Billy could not help but find it rather amusing that Frodo Fatlips sported a jet-black beard over thin, livery lips, while Ravenbeard had no facial hair at all but had lips as plump as marshmallows.

"We come from a land far, far away," continued Gringo. "A once beautiful land where we lived happily in peace and harmony. But that is no longer the case. A dark magic now creeps through our world. It grows by the day, bringing evil and peril to all."

Ravenbeard happily took up the story. "Since time began, we bobbits have been awaiting this danger, for it is spoken of in...

"The prophecy," quickly snapped Frodo Fatlips, who feared being left out of it all.

A dirty look was immediately cast his way by Ravenbeard before he continued. "However, the prophecy also speaks of a child from a land not of our own who possesses the ability to banish this evil from our world and save us all. And that is why we are here. For you see, you…"

"….are the Chosen One!" blurtec out Frodo Fatlips again, the weight of holding in these magnificent words proving too heavy to bear.

Ravenbeard's face instantly turned as black as Frodo Fatlip's beard. "That was my line, you gogginbotter!" he said, firmly crossing his arms and turning his back on his interrupting companion.

Gringo tutted a disapproving tut. "Such language in front of the child," he said, exasperated by the shenanigans of his fellow bobbits. After giving a stern look to his companions, he once more took up the story, which had now been tossec around more times than an old frisbee. "So, your Excellency, without you our task is hopeless, but with you by our side we will surely prevail. Therefore, we ask you to come with us. Please Sire, enter the portal and return with us to our realm to vanquish this evil and save our world!"

Billy sat in his bed wondering if this was all real. This sort of thing only happened in books, not to ordinary boys living ordinary lives. He pinched himself. No - this was not a dream! So, what was he to do? This was a big decision. He knew nothing of these bobbits - could they be trusted? He knew nothing of the quest - would it be dangerous? Would it be hard? Would it be long? There was so much to consider. These concerns seemed to be sensed by Gringo, who set immediately to put his mind at rest.

"Sire, if you are worried about life back here on Earth while you are gone, then fear not! Time between our realms is wildly different, so you can complete this mission and be back in your bed before the sun has risen on the new day. We beg you to come with us, your Excellency. Our world depends on you."

Billy had made up his mind. Thoughts of his nagging Mum comparing him to Curtis was what had tipped the scales. Billy knew that this was it. This was his chance to prove that Curtis is not the be all and end all, the bee's knees, the cat's pajamas, the cow's flip flops.

"I'm in," he said.

The bobbits embraced each other and jumped around in circles, like overly excited children on Christmas morning. "Come then, Chosen One, let us travel back to our land. There is much to prepare before we begin our great quest."

Billy hopped out of bed. He sniffed the armpits of his top that lay crumpled on the floor, before throwing it over his head. Then he yanked his jeans up to his waist and crammed his feet into his dirty shoes, twisting them around until his heels fell into place. "Okay, I'm ready to rock!"

Gringo moved away from Billy's bed. While his feet looked large and cumbersome, he walked as silently as a deer padding over snow. Upon reaching the corner of the room he gestured to the wardrobe. "Come then, O Great One. Walk into the portal in your wardrobe and enter our realm."

Billy started sniggering. "A portal in the wardrobe? Next, you'll be telling me that there's a lion and a witch in there."

Gringo frowned and a confused look moved across his porcine face. "Why would a lion and a witch be in a wardrobe? Isn't it a wooden cupboard for clothes, and clothes alone?"

"Yes, it is. But there is a book called the Lion, the Witch and the Wardrobe. It's written by..."

"A book about a lion and a witch living in a wardrobe?" questioned Gringo, cutting Billy off. "That doesn't make sense. Why would a lion and a witch live in a wardrobe? There would be no room. And lions and witches are not allies; would the lion not just devour the witch? Or a skilled witch could surely cast a spell on the lion to make his teeth and claws fall out?"

"No, you don't understand," said Billy. "They don't live together in the wardrobe. Some children find a portal in their wardrobe, and when they enter it, they meet a lion and a witch."

Gringo shook his head, looking disgusted at the very idea. "This sounds like a truly terrible book. I do not wish to read it at all." Then, returning to the matter in hand, Gringo moved over to the wardrobe and opened the door. He only pulled the handle with the faintest of touches, but the wardrobe door threw itself open as if alive and wildly excited - after years of doing nothing except storing clothes- to finally have a chance to shine. And shine it did, for as the door opened, an explosion of light burst free, and the room was awash in strange luminous colours. Inside the wardrobe appeared to be a waterfall of light, (perhaps called a lightfall?) except in this waterfall the light streamed upward (so perhaps it would be better named a lightrise?), culminating in a frothy mass of bubbles on the roof. The colours produced by the lightrise were extraordinary, the likes of which Billy had never seen. At the bottom was kind-of-like lime green, which changed at the top to nearly-but-not-quite blue.

Then, a still sulking Ravenbeard hopped into the wardrobe. The light engulfed him as if it were a living entity swallowing a mouthful of prey, and in no time at all, the bobbit had disappeared out of view. Next, Frodo Fatlips clambered in.

"Come with me," said Gringo. In mere moments we will be in our land."

Billy could not believe all this was happening. What an adventure, he thought taking Gringo's hand and stepping into the closet. Immediately, a technicolour tornado began swirling around him, which proved far too bright to bear, so he squeezed his eyes tightly shut. The tornado then seemed to squeeze Billy and for a few seconds he found it hard to breathe. The floor of the wardrobe trembled and shook, and Billy sensed that he was not in his bedroom anymore and that he was somewhere else entirely.

"Oh, I should introduce myself," said Billy, trying to distract himself from the butterflies he felt fluttering around in his tummy.

"There is no need, Sire," replied Gringo. "I know it already. Everyone in our world knows your name. It is taught in every school, preached in every church and discussed across every dinner table throughout the land. After all, you are our Saviour. You are the Chosen One. You are...Curtis Hennig!"

Somewhere Else Entirely

"Sorry, what do think my name is?" asked Billy, as the trembling of the floor beneath him eased and the light around him began to taper off into the atmosphere.

"Curtis Hennig. That is correct, isn't it? You are Curtis Hennig who lives at number 36 Wessington Avenue?"

Billy paused for a moment. He felt somewhat flummoxed, which soon gave way to annoyance!

Curtis blooming Hennig. Of course. Of course, he was the Chosen one. Why would it have been plain old disappointing Billy Baggins? But Billy could not tell the bobbits they had made a mistake. And anyway, why should he? Anything Curtis could do he could do too. Couldn't he?

"Um, yeah that's me alright. Curtis Hennig is my name and 36 is my house number. You've got the right guy," he said, hoping that he was more accomplished at lying than he was at most other things.

Gringo smiled. "Thank goodness," he said. "I thought for a minute I had made a mistake, although I was sure we were at number 36. I am not chief scout and finder for nothing!"

By now the light had completely faded and Billy found himself stood in a large hut. The room was sparse. A thick oak table and accompanying chairs seemed to be the only furniture of note and the windows were nothing more than circular holes cut into the dark and unappealing clay walls. Yet, the place felt inviting. Colourful tapestries hung from the walls and crackling away in the corner of the room blazed an open fire that warmed the space well. A deep rich smell from the burning timber perfumed the room, reminding Billy of visiting his Grandparent's countryside home on those harsh days in winter.

"Come," said Gringo, "let me introduce you to our leader."

Gringo scuttled off through a large arch, re-entering moments later with another bobbit in tow. This bobbit looked like a leader. He appeared taller than the others. He was certainly rounder! While the other bobbits were plain and unadorned, this stately creature wore a long-felt robe and an ornate golden chain dangled from his neck, so that when he walked, he jingled and jangled like a pocketful of loose change. But when he caught sight of young Billy standing in the centre of the room, he stopped pacing forward and froze on the spot.

Gringo gladly did the introductions. "Potrab, this is the Chosen One!"

Suddenly Potrab stomped over to Billy, his belly wobbled and jiggled like a jelly sat on an old tumble drier. The great bobbit clamped Billy's slight shoulders with his broad hands and gazed intently at him in the way a young child browses the shelves of a sweet shop. "A thousand blessings. This is indeed a wonderous day!" bellowed the grand bobbit.

Billy looked at the doe eyed creature in front of him. All this attention was something he was not used to, and it was making him feel a little uneasy.

"Um, it's nice to meet you, Potrab," he said, thrusting out his hand in an invitation to shake it. "My name is Billy."

Potrab and Gringo immediately turned to look at each other, anxious looks etched upon their piggy faces.

"Billy? But you are Curtis, are you not?" fretted Potrab.

"Oh...of course I am," said Billy, thinking quickly. "It's just that in our land people often shorten their names. For example, Benjamin is shortened to Ben, Daniel is Dan and Curtis is....um, Billy."

Potrab looked around the room as if an explanation for this strangeness could be plucked out of the air. "This is confusing to us bobbits, but as the Chosen One wishes - Billy it is."

Potrab clapped his shovel hands and immediately Ravenbeard and Frodo Fatlips, who had been stood motionless in the corner of the room since Billy's arrival, scuttled over.

"Go and tell all in the village that from henceforth the Chosen One is to be called Billy. Anyone who calls the Chosen One Curtis will have their tongue cut from their mouth."

The bobbits scampered off like a nut hunting squirrel.

"Don't worry too much," said Billy. "I would like to be called Billy, but there's no need to cut anyone's tongue out."

Seeming to completely disregard that last statement, Potrab returned his attention toward Billy. He squinted his eyes to keenly study the boy stood before him. Then he moved his head in so close that Billy felt Potrab's breath warm his face. It smelt like a cabbage that had sat for far too long in a pot of boiling water.

"Hmm," said Potrab, stroking his bristly chin, "something confuses Potrab? I thought the scriptures stated that the Chosen One was handsome?"

"Yes Sir, I was surprised too when I saw him," replied Gringo. "His eyes are very close together and his nose is akin to a tooba bulb."

Potrab shook his head. "No, no. It's more like a frong!" he stated with great authority.

"What's a tooba bulb and a frong?" Billy asked.

"A tooba bulb is similar in appearance to what you humans call an onion. A frong is like an earth potato, only more gnarled and held in a more unsightly skin," said Potrab, before continuing. "And the Chosen One's hair is supposed to be of golden silk, but in fact it could be mistaken for the nest of a clawed barnabus!"

"Okay," said Billy, running his fingers through his hair to remove some of the many knots, "enough of that. Look, I may not look like Brad Pitt to you guys but trust me, I am handsome. On Earth I am a total babe magnet."

Potrab and Gringo had no reason to disbelieve this, so talk moved back to the quest.

"So, your Excellency," said Potrab, "tomorrow you will begin on your quest. But tonight is not a night to be talking of such things. Tonight, is a night for celebration!" With that, Potrab walked over to the corner of the room and threw open two large wooden doors that opened out onto the village square. A huge party was already in full flow. A huge fire blazed in the middle of the square and around it bobbits sat on wooden crates drinking strange smelling concoctions from dull tin tankards, which they clinked together in time to the rhythm of the traditional bobbit songs, which they sang with hearty gusto. On the cobbled streets, young bobbits frolicked and played, and love-sick couples danced hand in hand under the light of the two great red moons that hung over head like huge blood oranges.

But as Potrab and Billy moved out of the hut and into the square, the music, the chatting, the dancing, the drinking - *everything* stopped. Everything fell silent. Everything was still. Billy looked around. A sea of bobbits' eyes were glued upon him. It was as if he was the sun and they were the planets, fixed in his orbit. The moment lingered for an age. Just Billy looking at the bobbits and the bobbits looking back at him.

Then, Potrab spoke.

"Yes bobbits, this is him. This, is the Chosen One!"

Suddenly a tremendous roar erupted and lifted into the sky. Bobbits rose from their crates and clapped their hands with unnecessary force before they all embraced each other like long lost family.

"Come," said Potrab, placing his furry arm around Billy's shoulder, "there is much to see. Let me show you around."

The Great Feast

Potrab led Billy through the crowd of rejoicing bobbits, who clamoured around him to try and touch and thank him, over to the edge of the square where a large canvas gazebo was erected. As they approached, Billy noticed a bobbit dressed in a once-white apron and tall chef's hat scurrying around. He was barking orders at other bobbits, who chopped and mixed and stirred at a blistering pace. Three enormous cauldrons bubbled behind the busy bobbits and trays full of strange and unusual looking ingredients were piled high on the workstations surrounding them.

"This is Ramsay," said Potrab, upon reaching the tent. "He is the finest chef in the land. He will be accompanying you on your quest. He will nourish you and give you strength in battle. But tonight, he prepares a great feast in your honour."

Ramsay, who was dripping in sweat and whose face was the colour of a perfectly ripe strawberry, took

Billy's hand in both of his and shook it furiously, as if it had a powerful electric current running through it.

"A pleasure, Sire," he said excitedly. "I have been training my whole life to feed the Chosen One and tonight I am cooking up my most ambitious, challenging, and delicious feast ever! Among the highlights are a stew of frongs, lightly poached in the nectar of a biscuss bush, a frinbow terrine seasoned with the resin of rare mountain garrots, and a griptoe samush! All these dishes are traditional bobbit dishes - a simple plant-based food, with every ingredient respected and sourced responsibly."

Billy looked around at the bowls of thick, gloopy mush being assembled before him. The smell of stewed vegetables sat strong in his nostrils. "It looks great," said Billy, "and I'm sure it is absolutely delicious, but I'm kind of a fussy eater – I don't suppose you have any Monster Munch?"

Ramsay looked at Billy. His eyes welled and his bottom lip trembled. "You…. don't want to eat my food," he said, choking back the tears.

"I may have a nibble later," said Billy, "but my heart is kind of set on Monster munch. You know how it is when you get a craving for something."

Potrab put a firm hand on Ramsay's shoulder. "Do not be upset, Ramsay. The Chosen One will have ample opportunity to taste your delightful food, but he is unused to our cuisine, and it appears he enjoys eating other things. And it should come as no surprise that he feasts on monsters."

"No, Monster Munch aren't actually made of monsters," said Billy. "They're a baked corn snack - kind of like crisps."

"Well, whatever they are, if the Chosen One wants them, then the Chosen One shall have them."

Once again, Potrab clapped his hands together and instantly, from seemingly out of nowhere, a bobbit appeared. "Go and fetch Gringo. And be quick in your pace!"

As the bobbit hurried off, Potrab pulled a glowing orb from the deep pocket of his chic satin robe and held it aloft. "This orb contains a rare and special magic. Inside contains the power to create a doorway from one realm to another. This is how we reached you, Billy."

Billy looked at the orb that Potrab held in his palm. It was beautiful. The same colours Billy had seen in his wardrobe danced around the outside of the orb, like a gasoline rainbow swirling on top of a puddle of water.

Suddenly the bobbit, who Potrab had sent away only moments ago, returned. With him was Gringo and a motley crew of other bobbits.

"You called for me, Potrab?" said Gringo.

"Indeed!" boomed Potrab. "You must return to the realm of the Chosen One and gather the monster munchers food that he desires."

With that, Potrab released the orb from his grasp, and it tumbled downwards. Upon hitting the floor, the delicate casing shattered into a thousand pieces and the bright lights within it poured upwards. Without hesitation, Gringo stepped in and instantly vanished into the light. He was immediately followed by another two bobbits.

Billy was about to ask Potrab a question, but before he could speak the words, Gringo was once again stood in front of him, holding a multipack of Monster Munch.

"Sire, we have your monsterous munchers," he said, thrusting them into Billy's hand. He paused. "Sadly, my fellow bobbits perished on this quest to please the Chosen One. But they died a noble and a happy death in knowing that the Chosen One has the food he requires."

A wave of sadness swept over Billy.... Gringo had got roast beef flavour - he was hoping for pickled onion!

.... And of course, he also felt a bit upset about the bobbits dying.

As Billy stood there feeling blue, Gringo began to snigger.

"Only.... joking," said Gringo, managing to speak through his bursts of laughter. "We retrieved the snacks from the house you humans call, Tesco. It was no big deal - the others are fine. Come on out, comrades."

One at a time, the bobbits clambered out of the light, a silly goofy smile plastered on their faces. They too were clearly amused at this *hilarious* practical joke.

"Yeah, very funny," said Billy in a monotone voice.

"Yes, that was indeed highly amusing," said Potrab, who did not seem to register Billy's sarcastic tone. "Gringo was once the court jester of our village, before becoming the chief seeker. He will be useful to you in many ways on your journey."

"Yeah, I'm sure he will," said Billy "Anyway, how did yyi get the crisps so fast? You were only gone for a few seconds."

"Our realms are very different," said Potrab. "Time passes much, much slower in your world. That is why you will be here many weeks, months even, but when you return home, it will still be the night you left. Your Mum will not even notice you gone."

"So, I won't miss school on Monday?" asked Billy.

"Certainly not. We know how much the Chosen One loves school, so we timed our arrival so that you wouldn't miss any."

"Thanks for that," said Billy, scratching his throat. "Do you know what? - I am a bit thirsty too. I don't suppose you could pop back to Earth and fetch me a can of Fanta, could you?"

"Apologies, Sire," said Potrab, "but no! We had but three orbs. Making them requires mixing many a rare ingredient, like a hair plucked from a unicorn's mane and the pollen of a Lorrainium - a beautiful plant that only flowers once every hundred years. Once we obtained and combined all the precious ingredients, it then takes many further months to develop the magic contained within the orbs. And then, we only had enough magic to create three orbs. Now, only one remains. This orb must be saved to return you home at the end of your quest."

Potrab put his furry arm around Billy's shoulder. "Come now, Billy, let us leave Ramsey to finish the feast and Gringo to prepare for tomorrow. I will continue to show you around. We still have much to see and do before you begin your great quest."

The Fellowship

Billy was exhausted. After a long night of meeting and greeting enthusiastic bobbits, he had only had a few hours in which to sleep. Even then he had barely slept a wink. The bed that he had slept on was made of a very coarse wool. So rough in fact, that Billy felt as if he had spent the night tossing and turning over a cheese grater. But it was not just the uncomfortable sheep wool bed that had kept him awake. The anxiety about what trials and dangers may lay ahead swirled around his head like the milky froth in a mug of hot chocolate. And then, when he had finally drifted into the land of nod, Potrab had woken him abruptly and dragged him from the warmth of his hut into the biting cold air of the misty morning where he was led out of the village and onto a nearby hillside. Billy was freezing and his socks and the bottom of his jeans were soaked though, for the long wild grass was sopping with dew, a hint that the first frosts would soon be here.

As Billy stood shivering, a band of bobbits popped up from over the hill, marching purposefully toward them. The four bobbits wore more clothing than yesterday. Each sported a thick fur coat and carried a huge rucksack on their back that bristled and bursted at the seams. Gringo struggled under the weight of two bags. The handle of a lute and some arrows protruded from one of them, and Billy knew that this bag was meant for him. Eventually, the bobbits arrived at where Billy stood, and it was then down to Potrab to address the crew.

"O Chosen One, allow me to introduce you to the crew who are to accompany you on your great quest. Some you have already met. Gringo, the bobbits' chief scout and finder, knows the land like no other. Anywhere you need to go, he knows the way. He knows all shortcuts and every peril that lies around each corner. Ramsey is the finest chef in our realm. He will nourish you on your journey, provide you with wholesome and delicious meals that will fuel you on your adventure.

This bobbit is Joggan," said Potrab as he pointed to a nerdy looking bobbit with glasses. "He is an expert in the word of the prophecy. He knows the history and legend of our realm like the back of his hand. He will advise you wisely in the trials that await.

And finally, we have Barry."

"And what does Barry do?" asked Billy, looking over to the grinning bobbit.

"Nothing really," said Potrab. "Barry is here in case you wish to hone your fighting skills. We searched our people to find the bobbit with the largest, roundest head that would make the best punching bag. That bobbit is Barry."

Barry scuttled up to Billy. "Please punch me in my face, Sire" he said, squeezing his eyes tightly shut and sticking out the chin on his melon ball head, as if eagerly awaiting a blow.

"No, I don't want to punch you, Barry," said Billy, who was shocked at the very idea.

"Please, Master. It would be a great pleasure to feel the Chosen One's angry fists on my face," Barry pled.

"No, Barry. I really don't want to!"

"Barry, please!" interrupted Potrab. "The Chosen One obviously feels well equipped in battle and has no need to punch you in the face at this time. However, Billy, if you do feel the need to punch someone in the face or kick someone in the bottom during your quest then Barry is your bobbit," said Potrab, who grabbed Barry and roughly turned him around before pointing at his bottom, to indicate where Billy could kick. If he so wished.

Billy looked at Barry's large posterior and then again at his goofy smiling face. This was perhaps going to be a highly unusual quest, he thought to himself.

"Now," said Potrab, "I wish you every luck on your quest. It will be long, and it will be hard. Many of you will undoubtedly be injured - you may be spiked on spears, poisoned, burnt by raging fires or even tortured until you die a horrible, slow and painful death. But with the Chosen One at our side, we will surely succeed!"

"Thank you Potrab for the kind words," said Gringo. "I, for one, am excited about the quest ahead and I am ready to face every challenge that awaits us."

Billy did not share these sentiments. He felt more than a bit wobbly. For the first time since he arrived, the fog of doubt was beginning to cloud his mind. He began nibbling nervously on his fingernails, and he was happy to find a faint meaty taste from the monster munch still lingering. Could he do this? Could Billy achieve what Curtis Hennig was destined to achieve? Billy was not sure. If he was to confess to not being the Chosen One, then this was surely the time to do so. But there was only one orb left. Billy knew that if the bobbits used it to send him home and fetch Curtis instead, Curtis would not be able to return home for at least a hundred years. It was true that Billy had no time for Curtis, but to leave him stranded here, in this world, for that long seemed plain cruel. Billy's thoughts went back and forth and to and fro, but he had to decide. And that decision was that he was going to stay. Why couldn't he do it? Just because Curtis had been star of the week in school for a record one hundred and seventy-three weeks in a row, that did not mean that Billy hadn't special qualities of his own that might come in useful. Billy stood upright and puffed out his chest, as Potrab finished his speech.

"Billy and my fellow bobbits, you have a long, long way to travel, so you should begin. I wish you every luck on your quest. After all, our world depends on you!"

Billy and his band of bobbits took a step forward. The first step on a wild and exciting journey into the unknown.

Suddenly, Gringo stopped.

"I think I may need the toilet before we start," he said. So off he toddled, behind a bush, returning moments later looking refreshed and at ease. Billy and his band of bobbits then took another step forward - the second step on a wild and exciting journey into the unknown. Then the party took a third step, and then a fourth and – *well, you get the picture* - they continued to stride down the hill, away from the village.

"So where are we going?" asked Billy. "What's the first thing to do on our quest?"

"First," said Gringo, "we journey through Longwood Forest."

Joggan continued, "Sire, the journey through Longwood Forest will not be easy and it is not the quickest route. But to succeed in our quest we must surely speak with the Tree of Knowledge. You see it is he, and only he, that knows the name of the guardian of the key of Grainter. And we need this information to obtain the key, for it unlocks the door to the room that houses the sword of destiny!"

The Prophecy

"Hang on a minute," said Billy "The Tree of Knowledge, the guardian of the key of Grainter, the sword of destiny. What's all that about?"

"Your Excellency allow me to regale you with the history of our land," said Joggan, as the party paced across field and dale. "Let me tell you how our world came into being. How the Gods and Goddesses deemed our land worthy of life and created all that we see before us. It was many, many years ago and the moon of Salindor was perfectly in line with the sun of…."

"Sorry, Joggan," Billy said, yawning. "It sounds really interesting, but if you could just give me the low down then that'll be great. You know, just the essentials."

"Ah, I understand," said Joggan. "The Chosen One wishes to conserve his energy for the road ahead. An incredibly wise decision, Sire. Very well, I shall make it concise. At the dawn of time, seven Gods and

Goddesses came to our barren land and created all that there is. They created the moon, the stars and all the wonderful creatures - like us bobbits. Once they had finished and saw that their work was good, they returned to the realm of the Gods. But before they left, they each blessed a precious stone with their spirit and hid them in secure locations across our world. These spirit stones contain a great power - they sustain our land; they guide us and protect us. The stones have been hidden since the dawns of time. However, legend has it that one day an evil wizard of extra-ordinary power would be born, who would one day gain a powerful dark magic that would enable him to see the location of the stones. This is potentially disastrous as it is said that if an individual were to possess all the stones, then they will be able to open a door, deep within the misty mountains - the doorway to the realm of the Gods. It is said that whoever opens this door will then gain the power of the Gods and will be able to shape the world as they see fit. We believe that Lord Mouldywart, the ruler of the cave-dwellers, is this powerful wizard!"

"So, is he the guy I must defeat?" asked Billy. "What do you know about him?"

Lord Mouldywart is somewhat of an enigma. While he rules a group of cave-dwellers, most believe him to be of elven descent. But then, if this s true, he is an elf quite like no other. The story goes that one day a family of elves were awoken by a knock at the door. When they opened it, what appeared to be a baby elf, wrapped in a blanket, was upon the doorstep. No elf knew of his parents, or where he came from, but the family took him in believing him to be one of their own. However, as time passed and the child grew, it became clear that he was an evil and spiteful creature who took pleasure in the misfortune of others. He once said, "No!" to his parents and one day at elf-school he put a booger in the teacher's sandwich. The final straw was when he called one of the elders a 'poopy-pants!' The elves could take no more of this creature, so he was banished to the caves of Craggindor, where he was taken in by the cave-dwellers. Fuelled by anger, Lord Mouldywart began to learn the ways of dark magic and after gaining in power he began leading these creatures. Little else is known of Lord Mouldywart, but we believe that he already has several of the sacred stones in his possession. We think this as things are not right in our realm. A sickness spreads across our land like a virus. Plants are withering, animals dying. Devastating storms rage in the western isles and earthquakes ruin cities in the Eastern provinces. And just look at that," said Joggan, pointing to an empty monster munch packet that tumbled across the landscape like tumbleweed across the desert sands. "That litter is surely the work of Lord Moldywart! Therefore, we must attempt to find at least one of the sacred stones – this will prevent Lord Mouldywart from entering the chamber of the Gods. And that is why you must speak with the Tree of Knowledge. The Tree of Knowledge is the only one who can tell us the location of the remaining stones. The Tree of Knowledge knows all. He has slept since the dawn of time, but the prophecy states that he will speak with a human child and grant him the answers to questions, three! So, if you ask him for the location of at least one of the stones then we can retrieve it and Lord Mou dywart will be unable to open the door."

"But what if he has all the stones already?" asked Billy.

"Fear not. Even if Lord Mouldywart has all seven stones in his possession, there is still hope. Before leaving our land, the Gods and Goddesses also provided bestowed a sacred power in a sword in case the stones should ever fall into the wrong hands. This is the sword of destiny. The sword also resides in the heart of the misty mountains and legend has it that once someone has all the scared stones then only way to stop them from opening the chamber of the Gods is by slaying them with this mystical sword. But this sword is locked in a room and the only way to open it is with a magical key – the key of Grainter! But even once the door is opened, only the Chosen one will be able to pull the sword from the stone it is encased in and wield its power. You, Billy, are the only one who could use this powerful sword."

"Sounds intense," said Billy.

"Indeed, Sire. It certainly won't be easy, but whatever happens on the road ahead - we all believe in you," said Joggan reassuringly.

The other bobbits nodded in agreement.

"Come," said Gringo, "let us quicken our pace. The road is long, and we have little time."

The Tree of Knowledge

It had been four days. Four days of nothing but walking. Walking and talking. Walking, talking, and eating horrible vegetable stews. Billy had been rationing his monster munch but was now down to his final two packets. Soon he would surely be forced into eating Ramsay's disgusting concoctions. Life as part of the band of travelling bobbits was getting tedious. Billy felt that if Barry asked him to punch him in the face one more time, he may indeed do it! Being the Chosen One was not as exciting and rewarding as Billy had initially thought that it was going to be. In fact, it was quite the opposite! It had been just days of trekking through nothing but gnarled, dead trees and Billy had had to listen to the bobbits continually moan and groan about how the dark magic was beginning to penetrate and kill the beautiful forest, over and over and over again!

But in the past few hours some splashes of green had begun popping up on the trees and bushes as the power of the dark magic lost its hold, and now, as they party continued weaving through the dense maze of trees, the forest had seemingly burst into life – which had somewhat cheered the mood.

"I am so excited, Sire, because it is not much further until we reach the Tree of Knowledge," said Gringo.

Joggan, as usual, piped in with more boring details. "The ancient tree was the first thing that grew in our land all those moons ago. It is the only living being to have seen the Gods and Goddesses before they returned to their spiritual realm. The tree has witnessed all since the birth of our land and therefore knows everything. Prophecy says that he will answer any three questions of the Chosen One's desire. The answer to these questions will surely prove vital to the quest ahead. Now, Your Excellency, what you ask the tree is up to you, however, it will surely be useful to know the location of at least one of the spirit stones so

48

we can retrieve it. And I also feel compelled to remind you that to enter the room that holds the sword of power we need the magical key of Grainter. The key has been protected by a guardian in the swamps of Wiffindor for thousands of years. Legend states that the guardian will only hand over the key to an individual who can state his name. We need to know the guardian's name!"

"No worries," said Billy, trying to act cool. "I'll ask about the stone and I'll find out what the dude's name is."

Suddenly Gringo thrust out his arm in front of the party, indicating that they should stop.

"The Tree of Knowledge is but a few hundred metres down there," said Gringo, pointing through the gaps in the trees with his outstretched finger.

The party all stood silent and still, looking at Billy. Waiting.

"You guys aren't coming?" Billy asked.

"No, Your Excellency," said Joggan. "The Tree of Knowledge will not wake in the presence of us undeserving bobbits. He will only talk to a human, and a human alone. Also, the Chosen One needs to deeply focus on the questions and the crucial information that the tree provides. Us bobbits will only prove a distraction."

"Okay, I'll see you in a while then, "said Billy. He then began sheepishly weaving in and out of the trees, pushing back the gnarled, twisted branches that seemed intent on blocking his way.

After a few minutes, Billy noticed a clearing up ahead. Making his way toward it, his eyes were instantly drawn to the colossal tree that stood solitary in the centre of the clearing. It was easily the biggest tree Billy had ever seen. It was easily the biggest tree that *anyone* had ever seen. It was as wide as a bus. And it was tall. It stretched so high into the sky that Billy had to crane his neck back to the point of it hurting to see the leafy canopy, which was so sprawling, that it acted like a giant umbrella, shielding out every single ray of the shimmering sun. Billy stood under the heavy shade of the tree and called out, "Hello?"

Nothing! Had Billy got the right tree? It surely had to be. But then, why was it not responding?

"Hello, Tree of Knowledge. It is the Chosen One here. I would like to ask you some questions please." said Billy politely.

Suddenly a huge crack exploded from within the tree and echoed through the forest. The ground beneath Billy shook violently. The bark on the tree then began to loudly splinter, and, as it tore open, features began to emerge from the wood. Large, brown eyes and a gaping mouth became ever more pronounced, until a clear vision of an old, wise tree-bark face was looking down upon the small and meek child stood in front of it.

"Are you, the Tree of Knowledge?" Billy asked, a slight tremble in his voice.

The tree's lips moved slowly and deliberately. "I am," it replied, in a deep booming voice. "Are you he?"

"Yes, I am he," said Billy, hoping that the Tree of Knowledge was not wise enough to see through his ever-expanding web of lies. "I am Curtis Hennig - the Chosen One."

"Hmmm," the tree mused, as it adjusted his long-time-unused eyes to gain better sight of Billy, "I thought you were supposed to be handsome?"

"I am handsome, "snorted Billy, immediately wishing to change the subject before hearing that his nose looked like another type of root vegetable. "So, what's your name?"

"I have no name. I am known simply as the Tree of Knowledge," replied the tree in a lyrical lilt. The way the tree spoke was highly unusual. The pitch of his voice seemed to be riding upon a wave, as it slowly moved up and down and then back up again. It seemed to be singing the sentences rather than speaking them.

"I know all about this great and," continued the tree, "and I feel it to be dying. I feel my strength diminishing with each passing day. You must be quick in completing your task the sands of time are running out."

"Don't worry, Tree of Knowledge," replied Billy in an encouraging tone. "I'm going to smash this quest. Right, let us get down to business. Can I ask you a question?"

"You just did," the tree replied.

"I didn't," said Billy. "What question?"

"You asked if you could ask me a question? That, is a question."

Billy paused for a moment.

What an idiot! That *was* a question. One vital question completed and utterly wasted! Billy stood still and thought very carefully about what his next question was going to be. He had to be completely sure of the next words that came out his mouth.

"Can you tell me the location of one of the spirit stones?"

"I cannot," said the tree solemnly.

"Why not?" Billy asked. "You're the Tree of Knowledge, aren't you? I thought that you knew everything?"

The tree slowly rolled its eyes like marbles on a tray. "I do know everything, but your three questions are answered." The tree's mouth opened wide, and a gigantic yawn spilled forth. "I grow weary now, child. I need to rest."

"What do you mean my three questions are answered? Alright, I may have wasted one, but I have two more left!"

The great tree puffed out his thick wooden cheeks and exhaled. The force of which sent Billy reeling backward.

"You asked if I was the Tree of Knowledge?

Then you asked my name?

And then you asked if you could ask a question?

I hope you find my answers of value on your quest. I wish you well, Curtis. After all, you are our only hope."

With that, the ground began rumbling again and the crack in the tree, which was its mouth, began to squeeze shut. The bark twisted and tightened around the eyes and just like that, he was gone!

Billy stood and looked up at the tree for a while in disbelief. He then began calling his name again and again and again to try and get him to come back. But it was useless. It was as useless as a normal child standing in a normal wood calling out to an ordinary elm or oak in the hope of it awakening. When he realised that there was no real hope in the Tree of Knowledge returning, Billy began trudging back through the forest to the band of bobbits, who sat eagerly awaiting his return.

"Sire, was it useful?" asked Joggan, leaping to his feet. "Did he tell you all you needed to know?"

"Um...Yeah, it was kind-of useful," said Billy coyly. He began to panic. Should he tell the bobbits the truth and confess to wasting his three wishes? He felt like he was falling further and further into a black hole, and the further he fell, the harder it was becoming to claw his way back out! But Billy knew that he now had no choice but to keep up the charade and plough on. It was he that was here, and it was impossible for Curtis to swoop in and save the day now. Billy knew that this quest was his and his alone. He promised himself then and there, that he would be much more careful in all future tasks. Billy felt hollow inside after wasting his three questions, but he clung for dear life onto the hope that maybe he could find a spirit stone and work out the guardian's name some other way.

"Did he say anything else?" asked Barry. "Did he mention me?

"Barry, cease!" said Joggan. "Sire, I'm sorry about Barry. Please feel free to punch him if you wish."

Barry closed his eyes and outstretched his chin.

"No thanks," said Billy. "Let's just keep going shall we."

"A wonderful idea, Sire," said Gringo. "So which way are we headed? Are we heading to find a stone, or does Lord Mouldywart possess them all already - which would then mean that we are heading to the swamps of Wiffindor to retr eve the key of Grainter, would it not?"

"Um…. Let us just head to the swamp and get the key. The Tree of Knowledge said there is a stone nearby as well, which we will pass on the way. I cannot say much more about it really. The tree said it is best to keep it all to myself. He said the more people know the more dangerous it is," he said, lying through his teeth.

"That sounds like an excellent plan," said Gringo. "Let us travel east then. The swamps cf Wiffindor await us!"

Camping under the Red Moons

Billy was exhausted. He had walked more in the last few days than he had in all his life. His feet were throbbing, and his blisters now had blisters - and they were beginning to get blisters, too! And boy was Billy hungry. So hungry that he was even thinking about eating some of vegetable kebabs that Ramsay was current roasting above the fierce open fire. As Billy sat on a gnarled log, looking into the flames that crackled and danced before him, he thought about home. He missed it. And with every minute that ticked by, he was regretting his decision to pose as Curtis more and more. But there was no going back now. He was stuck here with the bobbits on their great quest, whether he liked it or not.

With a nimble flick of the wrist, Ramsay turned the kebabs on the fire. He handled them with such care you would swear that they were precious gold ingots, not grubby, unearthed vegetables impaled on a stick.

Ramsay took great pride in his work, and he was clearly skilled, for not a single hunk of vegetable lined upon the kebab skewer was any other colour than perfectly-cooked-golden-brown.

"Only a few more minutes and the kebabs will be ready for consumption," said Ramsay, spinning the skewers like fine silk on a loom. "I so hope they please, the Chosen One."

The bobbits constant need to please him was driving Billy mad.

"I'm sure they'll be lovely," said Billy.

"If you do not like them Sire, then you can always take out your frustration out on me," said Barry, the light from the flames illuminating the curvature of his perfectly spherical head.

As Billy and the band of hungry bobbits sat awaiting their kebabs, their ears were suddenly drawn to the sound of rustling from the bushes at the edge of the campsite.

"Sssh," whispered Gringo, "Do you hear that?"

The gang sat in silence, straining their ears to listen for further sound. And then, suddenly from the edge of the camp, a pair of bright eyes shone out through the darkness of the trees. The eyes sparkled like distant stars in the night sky, before growing larger as a sleek dark shape crawled out of the foliage. The creature growled upon approach and, as it came ever closer, the flames of the fire showed it to be a huge, muscular wolf. The wolf stopped as it reached the edge of the campsite. It lowered its front legs and pulled its top lip back, aggressively displaying its sharp fangs to the party before it.

"Oh my, it's a shark," said Barry, quivering with fear.

"No Barry - sharks are the ones that live in the water. This is a wolf," explained Gringo, over the wolf's loudening growls.

"He looks hungry," said Ramsay, slowly moving his arm toward the fire and grabbing a vegetable kebab. He threw it in the direction of the wolf, in the hope that it would satisfy the creature. But the wolf did not even sniff at it! Instead, it began snarling even louder and began gnashing his teeth at Billy and the terrified bobbits.

"It doesn't want vegetables," said Gringo. "It wants meat. And we're the meat!"

The tension among the other bobbits did not seem to be shared by Joggan who, in contrast, appeared quite relaxed. "Legend has it that the Chosen One can talk to the animals," he said in a cool and calm manner. "Billy, please tame this beast."

Billy was stunned. Tame the beast? He was no match for the next-door neighbour's Jack Russell that terrorised him whenever he cycled around the estate, let alone this giant savage hound that loomed large before him.

And then Barry began to wail loudly.

"Please, Sire," he moaned. "I'm getting very scared. I have wet my tunic!"

Billy looked over to Barry. A long string of snot dangled precariously from the end of his nose, like a pendulum on an old grandfather clock. Barry looked back at Billy with wide hopeful eyes. In this moment, Billy realised that the bobbits were completely and utterly helpless. It was up to him to do something to help.

And then Billy suddenly remembered what his Uncle Joe used to do with his dog, Patches. Standing up, he slowly made his way over to the angry wolf, one hand outstretched and his fingers stretched open, to show he meant no harm.

Upon approach, the wolf began snarling and barking gruffly. It was ready to pounce!

Billy carefully reached into his trouser pocket with his free hand and rummaged around, before pulling out an empty pack of monster munch that he had eaten earlier in the day. "There you go, boy," offered Billy with a trembling hand, "have a taste of that." He tossed the packet into the air.

The wolf leapt up and snatched it in mid-air and proceeded to stuff his snout into the empty bag. Its tongue flicked furiously from its mouth as it cleaned the packet of every remaining pocket of favour.

"Quick," said Billy, looking at Joggan, "pass me my bag."

Joggan grabbed the bag and tossed it over. Billy hastily unzipped it and rooted inside. He pulled out his last packet of monster munch and, with some hesitation, tugged open the bag.

"Look, boy," he said, holding the packet open for the wolf to see, "there's more where that came from."

Billy turned the packet upside down and the large, baked corn snacks tumbled onto the floor. Instantly, the ravenous wolf buried his snout into the ground and greedily gathered up each and every one of the monster munch.

The gang stood and watched as the wolf finished the last paw shaped snack. It licked the ground clean of crumbs before raising its head. Billy stared at the wolf and the wolf stared at Billy. Time was frozen for what seemed like an eternity, before the wolf slowly turned and headed back into the forest. Soon, it was gone.

"You saved us, Sire," said Gringo.

Barry jumped to his feet and raced over to Billy.

"That was magnificent, Your Excellency," he said, flinging his arms round Billy and squeezing him so tightly that Billy had to wriggle and squirm around a good bit to catch his breath. Barry then began kissing Billy repeatedly - again and again and again. "Thank you, Sire. Thank you so much."

As if being kissed by a bobbit was not bad enough, Billy could feel the slimy snot from Barry's nose wiping against his face every time he moved in for another smooch.

"Barry, get off me," said Billy, still trying to bustle free.

Barry was not listening. He continued to peck at Billy's cheek like a woodpecker working on a tree trunk.

"Barry, if you don't get off me right now, I'm going to hit   you,"   threatened   Billy.

Immediately Barry released Billy from his grasp and lowered himself down to one knee.

"It would be my pleasure, O Chosen One," said Barry, closing his eyes in glorious anticipation.

Billy sighed. "No Barry, I don't want to hit you really. I just wanted you to get off me," he said, rubbing the mucus from his face with the sleeve of his top.

But it was not just Barry who was in awe of Billy at this moment. Even Joggan, who was normally so cool, calm and collected, was clearly highly emotional at the events that had just unfolded. He was trembling slightly, and his eyes were damp with tears. "What a glorious night," he said. "It was always said that the Chosen One can talk with the animals and here is the proof. The prophecy is coming into fruition!"

Billy smiled coyly. A mild blush warmed his cheeks. "I'm not sure about that," he said. "I'm just glad I could get rid of the wolf."

"Do not be modest, Sire," said Ramsay. "You were magnificent! Now, the Chosen One must be hungry after performing such a great feat. Come, eat," he said. Ramsay pulled a skewer from the fire and thrust it into Billy's hand. With the monster munch gone, Billy now had little choice but to eat the food Ramsay had prepared. So, he raised the skewer to his mouth and took a small bite, which was quickly followed by another larger one.

"Hey, that's actually pretty good, Ramsay."

A colour of ripe plum instantly exploded onto Ramsey's face as if he had been shot in the face with a purple paint pellet from a paintball gun.

"Sire, you are too kind," said Ramsey, as he began handing out the remaining kebabs to his hungry companions.

And then Billy and the bobbits sat around the fire, eating and chatting. Billy smiled to himself as he finished his kebab. Being here was not actually that bad and being the Chosen One was proving quite rewarding.

Ambushed

With the pleasant thoughts of last night's incident still fresh in the memory, the morning found Billy in good spirits. For the first time since he arrived, Billy found himself enjoying himself. Today his eyes were wide open to the world around him and the weird and wonderful wildlife that inhabited it. As the party ventured deeper and deeper into the forest, the more it sprang to life. While barren at the edges, Lord Mouldywart's dark magic had not yet spread to the heart of the forest and it was now teeming with strange creatures, the likes of which Billy had never seen. Billy had spent many minutes just observing the heartbeat of a delicate tree frog with a completely transparent skin. It was so beautiful. He could have stayed watching it all day, but unfortunately it was eaten by a hootinany - an animal a bit like a flying hedgehog. But around every corner was a new wonder to behold. It was incredible! Even the terrible song the bobbits had sang, all day and every day, as they trekked through the forest was not as grating today. Billy even found himself joining in!

"We are on a quest with the Chosen One. We are having so much fun!"

Today Billy was fully present in the world around him. His senses were tingling and as finely tuned as they had ever been in his whole life.

"What is the name of that bird, Joggan?" quizzed Billy, as a shrill whistle was heard overhead.

"I am unsure, Sire," said Joggan. "It is a call of which I am unaware. Let us listen, to see if we can hear it again."

Another whistle was heard.

Billy looked in all directions, to see if he could see for himself what manner of creature was making the noise. But instead of seeing the magnificent exotic bird he anticipated, he instead saw Joggan fall to the ground like a felled oak. Joggan's face smashed into the ground with a tremendous band and there he lay, motionless on the muddy ground. Quickly, the party gathered around.

"Joggan, are you alright?" asked Gringo, bending down and shaking him gently.

Joggan was not responding.

Gringo then yanked something from Joggan's neck. It was a small, sharp wooden dart with plumes of tight red feathers jutting out from all sides. And then, suddenly, another whistling sound flew past. It was followed by a thud; another dart lodging firmly in the tree trunk behind them. In a state of panic, the group scanned around to see where the dart had come from and saw, in the distance, a group of horrible looking creatures running through the trees towards them. They were ugly things with deep green leathery hides and small wrinkled heads that looked like kiwis that had been sat in a fruit bowl far too long. The foul creatures all had smears of bright paint streaked across their face with blow pipes pressed tightly against their mouths. And they looked determined on hitting more of the party with their poisoned darts.

"Goblins!" yelled Gringo. "Run!"

"What about Joggan?" said Billy. "We can't leave him."

"We must, "said Gringo, taking firm grasp of Billy's arm and pulling him away. "Protecting the Chosen One is all that matters. Joggan would agree."

At once, Billy, Gringo, Ramsay and Barry began running from the goblins, ducking and weaving through the branches of the trees, as a stream of darts continued to whizz past them.

"Run in front of me, Sire," said Barry. "My head will shield you from the darts."

Another flurry of darts zoomed past. How every one of them managed to avoid Barry's head beggared belief - it was surely easier for the goblins to hit such a large object than miss it, even with a wonky aim!

Soon the party found themselves at a woodland path, thick with trees on one side and a steep bank leading down to a small stream on the other.

"Quickly, slide down," ordered Gringo, stuttering down the slope as quickly as he could manage without tumbling down.

The other members of the party skipped and slipped down the mucky bank after him.

"Camouflage yourselves with mud and leaves," instructed Gringo.

Everyone led down in the ooze and rolled around to cover themselves from head to toe in deep, brown muck. Once sufficiently coated, Gringo hastily threw some nearby twigs and leaves over Billy, Barry and Ramsay, before joining them on the forest floor. And there they lay, perfectly still, looking up to the woodland path at the goblins who had stopped to look around for their prey. The longer Billy looked at the goblins, the more disgusting he found them to be. They looked like a pack of bulldogs sucking on super-sour gobstoppers. The goblins looked up the path and then down the side of the bank. Billy felt sure that one of the goblins would spot them.

But, after a minute or so of looking, one of the goblin's spoke up. "Blah rath a grinot mar postie," it said in a rasping voice. Then, half of the goblins continued to run down the woodland path and the other half turned and walked back where they came from."

Billy and the bobbits waited for several more minutes to make sure the goblins had gone. Billy then whispered to Gringo, "What did the goblin say?"

"My goblin tongue is not perfect, but I believe it said, "You lot go and find that bobbit with the large juicy head, while we return to camp and cook the bobbit we have."

"We cannot let that happen," said Billy. "We have to save Joggan!"

"We cannot risk being caught by those goblins," said Gringo. "If they catch you Billy, then our quest is over and the whole of our world will perish. Joggan would understand this, and he would not want you to rescue him. We cannot risk your life - you are too important!"

"No!" commanded Billy. "I am the Chosen One and what I say goes. We are going to save Joggan and we are going to do it now!"

Saving Private Joggan

Gringo stopped, he bent down to a plant and inhaled deeply. "The goblins passed through here, and not long ago. We are near."

"How do you know that just from smelling a leaf?" Billy asked.

"One of the goblins must have recently gone to the toilet. There is wee on the leaves. It is still warm. Come and feel for yourself."

"No, I'll take your word for it," said Billy. "Let's just keep going and get Joggan."

The party followed Gringo until eventually the goblin's campsite came into view. The gang ducked down behind a large row of bushes on the edge of the camp to conceal themselves from view. Billy and the bobbits peered through the gaps in the hedgerow to see what was going on. And there was Joggan! He was strung up by his legs, with his head dangling precariously over a huge metal cauldron. Underneath the pot a great fire was ablaze and the water that filled it was at a rolling simmer with thin wafts of steam beginning to gently rise into the air. One goblin was throwing and shaking all manner of items into the warming water and, as it did so, a pleasant smell of herbs and spices drifted delightfully through the forest air.

"Mmmmmm, it smells quite nice," said Barry.

Ramsay took great offense at this. "If you like the smell so much, why don't you join them and help eat Joggan - you traitor!"

Billy felt the need to calm the mood. "Relax, Ramsay. Let us think about how we are going to save Joggan."

"If I may be so bold, Sire," said Gringo. "I belief there to be a few options; firstly, the water in the pot may not yet be boiling! If you act right away and shoot through the rope with your bow and arrow, Joggan will fall in, and he may be able to clamber out and escape."

"But he might drown though," said Billy.

"Well, the second option is that you could shoot each and every last goblin. But, and as skilled as you are with the bow, Billy, that would still be an awfully hard task considering their number."

"Any more options?" said Billy. "I don't think really like either of those."

"Just one more," said Gringo.

Before telling Billy exactly what option number three entailed, Gringo attempted to get Joggan's attention.

"Psst!" he whispered.

It did not work, so he tried again, a little louder this time.

"Psst!"

This time Joggan heard. And when he looked to where the sound was coming from, he caught sight of Gringo in the bushes.

Gringo then began swinging his arm back and forth.

Joggan seemed to understand the instruction and began to wiggle his body around like a worm on a fishing hook. He only moved a little, at first, but he soon gained momentum and began to swing higher and higher and higher, like a carefree child on a swing.

When the goblins saw what Joggan was doing they began to get angry. They swarmed around the cauldron and started jabbing at Joggan's bottom with their sharpened sticks, to try and get him to stop.

Joggan bravely resisted and continued to swing higher and higher, back and forth.

Then Gringo thrust a bow and an arrow into the palm of Billy's hand. "Ready yourself, O Chosen One. This will be a tough shot - impossible for most - but for an expert archer like you, a shot of which you are more than capable of. When Joggan is at his highest point, you must shoot through the rope. He will fly in this direction, and we will quickly untie him and flee to safety. But you have only one shot to do this Billy, because once you release the dart the goblins will be aware of our presence. Our lives are in your hands."

In his hands? In his trembling and sweaty hands, Billy could barely fix the arrow into position, let alone execute such a precise shot under such enormous pressure. This was a disaster. It was all very well and good pretending he was the Chosen One when he did not have to do anything, but now, when it came to the crunch, it was not quite as easy. But Billy had no option but just to do his best. Drawing the bowstring back, Billy held it taught. He took aim and focused on the swing of the rope, following it back and forth, back and forth, back and forth. Billy continued following the swing of the rope. He was at one with the rope. He was the rope!

As Joggan swung toward him, Billy exhaled, and with that, released the bowstring. The arrow shot through the air like a, well.... like an arrow.

The party watched on tenterhooks as the arrow flew tantalisingly through the air towards the rope, before sailing straight past it by a good fifteen foot.

"You missed, Sire?" said Gringo, clearly confused.

Billy did not have a chance to respond. The arrow continued to fly through the air before it collided into a tree and ricocheted off onto another tree, where it buried itself into a large furry cocoon like object, which then plummeted downwards, landing squarely on a goblin's head, trapping its ugly mug inside.

Immediately, the goblin began to wail a muffled wail and flail its arms around in a state of panic. And then a large dark buzzing cloud seeped out from the cocoon.

"It's a sharks' nest," said Barry, excitedly.

"No, Barry," said Gringo, "It is a nest of tree hornets. Billy you are a genius!"

The hornets were furious at being disturbed. You could hear it in their angry buzzing. Hundreds and thousands of hornets continued to pour out of the nest and began to spread through the goblin camp stinging everything and anything in sight. It was like dominos - first one goblin started dancing around as the hornets began to sting it unmercifully, and then another and another and another, and in no time at all, the entire party of goblins were running around in a frenzy. It was chaos! Goblins were jumping up and down, bumping into each other, scratching themselves against trees and smacking at their clothing, all in a feeble attempt to rid themselves of the hornets. And then, some goblins began rolling around on the floor. And that is when one of them rolled onto the cooking pot, spilling the contents all over the forest floor.

One of the goblins began shouting, "Grreto thy aquar!"

"What's it saying?" asked Billy.

"I am unsure," said Gringo, "There are hornets in its mouth stinging it, but I think it is saying, 'to the stream."

In a state of panic, the goblins began dancing away to find water.

This was it. This was their chance. Billy and the bobbits darted out from behind the bush and ran toward Joggan. Ramsay grabbed a sword from Joggan's backpack that lay on the ground by the cauldron and thrust it into Billy's hand. Billy shimmied up the tree and hacked away at the rope that strung up poor Joggan. Suddenly the rope split and Joggan plummeted to the ground, where he was caught by

Ramsay, Barry and Gringo, who waited underneath. Billy clambered down from the tree and then he, and the bobbits, ran the opposite way to the goblins. After a period, when they felt safe, they stopped to catch their breath. As Billy knelt over in exhaustion, Joggan grasped both of his shoulders.

"Promise me you will never do that again," he said sternly. "You are never to endanger yourself for me, or any other bobbit. You are too important. Do you understand?"

Billy nodded.

"However," said Joggan, more calmly this time, "I am very grateful."

"But how did you spot that horret's nest?" Ramsay asked.

Billy was just about to concoct another lie, but Joggan did not permit him the time. "There is no time to talk; that was far too close for my liking. Let us continue to move forward and get out of this forest, once and for all."

The Elven Village

Billy was glad to be leaving the forest after further days of trekking through it. It had been a great adventure, and apart from wasting his three questions with the Tree of Knowledge, it had proven rather successful. Billy had seen a world of magic that he could never have imagined in his wildest dreams. However, all the walking and camping under the stars in the cold of the night with a group of bobbins, flatulent from eating too many frongs, had also been easily the most challenging experience of his young life – and that is without mentioning the wolf and the goblins!

"The elves and the bobbits have always been kindred spirits," said Joggan, as they continued to distance themselves from the trees behind them. "Our eleven friends will welcome us like long lost brothers. Tonight, we will feast and dance and rest in comfort on beds stuffed with the feathers of a bloose mongrab. And then tomorrow morn we will wake up refreshed and replenished and we shall begin our journey towards the swamp of Wiffindor."

Billy smiled. He was looking forward to sleeping in a bed and, despite growing accustomed to Ramsay's cuisine, he was looking forward to eating something other than boiled or roasted vegetables, even if it was for one night only.

As was always the way, Gringo led the party as they marched over the long, wet grass of the ultra-green fields. A cool breeze helped refresh their weary souls as they made their way up a small hill, the last obstacle that separated them from the elven village. The misty mountains, that contained the sword of destiny and the doorway to the Gods, were also now in view. The huge snow-covered mountain range shimmered and sparkled in the distance as if t were covered in diamonds - its beauty surely betraying the dangers that lay within.

"The village will soon be in sight," said Gringo, as they neared the summit of the hill.

"I'm excited," said Barry. "I've never been on holiday before!"

All the bobbits seemed excited. They seemed to be bouncing now rather than walking. But when they reached the top the hill and looked down on the village below, their joy instantly plummeted into the depths of despair.

Plumes of dirty black smoke and ash drifted up into the air from the charred husks of the burned-out houses below and the smell of acrid burnt timber began to make itself apparent to Billy and the bobbit clan.

"Quick, "said Joggan, "Something terrible has happened - the elves may be in danger!"

Everyone began running down the hill as fast as they could manage without tumbling down, until they reached the village at the bottom.

The elven village was surrounded by a thick wooden perimeter fence. It was coated in ash, as if a heavy black snowstorm had raged for days. Outposts were spaced evenly about twenty metres apart. All were unattended. A large gateway marked the entrance, and the gates were open so Billy and the bobbits walked straight through.

The stink of burn was now extraordinarily strong and deeply unpleasant, and Billy could feel the fierce heat emanating from the smouldering rubble of the burned-out houses around him. A few elves dashed around, throwing buckets of water on the steaming remains of their homes. They all seemed oblivious to the presence of the Billy and the bobbits. Cries, moans and wails came from every angle and Billy could feel an atmosphere of despair hanging in the air as the they marched into the village square.

"Landor? Griffit? Are you there my elven friends?" called Joggan, scanning around the decimated village for signs of life.

He called again, louder this time.

And then, the outline of a figure began to its way through the smoke. Its pale face was adorned with pristine, sharp features and a lock of shimmering white hair streamed down its face and rested on slight shoulders.

"Joggan, is that you?" said the elf, wafting smoke away from his stinging, bloodshot eyes.

"Yes, Landor it is I."

"It is good to see you, my friend. It is good to see all of you," said Landor, looking around the party of bobbits. "Your presence is a welcome light shining upon us in this terrible darkness."

"What happened here?" Joggan asked.

"A terrible tragedy has befallen out village," said Landor, his voice hoarse from the burn of smoke. "As you bobbits must have felt too, we elves have sensed a dark energy growing stronger within our world. But we never expected this!

I awoke in the middle of the night to the sound of a terrible crash. I, and other elves, vacated our huts to see what the noise was, and that is when we saw our beloved statue of the Gods and Goddess smashed into pieces upon the floor. There were cave dwellers everywhere and they seemed to be escaping through a hole in the ground at the edge of the square! We immediately took up arms and began to fight, but a handful of cave dwellers broke free and proceeded to set fire to our huts with flaming torches. It was chaos! Elves were fleeing from their houses screaming, elves were running back and forth to the well with buckets full of water, trying to douse the flames. All this while the battle raged on. Many cave dwellers were slayed, many escaped, but after it was all done, we investigated the tunnel from which the cave dwellers came and escaped from. We travelled through the tunnel. It must have been a couple of miles in length. It originates at the edge of Longwood Forest. The cave dwellers must have dug it to be able to enter our village without alerting our lookouts on the perimeter fence. They must have been digging the hole for many months to ambush us in this way. This darkness is long in the making and extra-ordinarily cunning in its execution."

"So, I am guessing that one of the spirit stones was within the statue of the Gods and Goddesses?" Joggan said. "Was this what the cave dwellers were after?"

"I presume so," said Landor. "That statue has stood since the dawn of time. It is said in eleven folklore that the first elves came upon the glorious statue as they walked across field and dale seeking a place to settle, and when they came upon the statue, they knew it was sacred and holy, so they decided to build their homes there – and thus, our great city was born! It has been said many times that a spirit stone resides in the statue, but no one knew for sure. Not until now, that is. And now it is gone, along with the fading hopes of all people across our world!"

With that, Landor collapsed to the ground, buried his head into his ghost-white hands and began to sob uncontrollably.

Joggan then looked at Billy. "Was this the stone the Tree of Knowledge told you of?"

Billy did not know what to say. After witnessing the tragic devastation of the elven city, and seeing the agony of this poor elf, he did not want to lie. But the piece seemed to fit perfectly into his jigsaw of lies, so he nodded. And he nodded because while nodding was still lying, it felt less awful than speaking the words.

"So, Lord Mouldywart has yet another stone. It is likely that he now has most, if not all of the stones, in his possession!" said Joggan. However, despite the terrible events that were unfolding before him, Joggan seemed somewhat upbeat. He returned his attention toward Landor. "I know things seem dark right now, but do not fear, dear friend, this plight on your people is only temporary. Your city will rise again. You see, our party contains someone incredibly special." Joggan paused, "Landor, this is the Chosen One!" And Joggan opened out his arm to indicate Billy's presence. "We will go immediately and retrieve the key of Grainter and obtain the sword of power. Then the Chosen One will destroy Lord Mouldywart at the gateway to the chamber of the Gods, and peace and harmony will once again return to our land."

Landor arose and wiped the tears from his eyes. He took Billy's hand and began kissing it. All his crying had made his nose all wet and snotty, like a dog, but Billy could not say anything - the poor elf's world had just been turned upside down.

"Sire, it is a great pleasure. It is a huge comfort knowing that you are here with us and are ready to fulfil your destiny. All our hopes reside in you now. But know that you are not alone. We elves will assist you on your quest. I, and my strongest elves, will accompany you into battle. We will leave tonight and head to the misty mountains and meet you at the door to the chamber of the Gods. Our swords of elven steel may help in the final battle w th Lord Mouldywart!"

"That is heartening to know," said Joggan, before turning to Billy "I am sorry, Billy. I know I promised you a comfortable bed for the night and a feast in your honour, but fate has decided that it is not to be. We must continue immediately. Lord Mouldywart has another stone. He may have gained all the stones by now, so we must quicken our pace. We need to obtain the key of Grainter, get the sword of power and reach the chamber of the Gods, as quickly as possible. Landor, I am sorry for the tragedy that has befallen your village, and I am sorry to abandon you in your hour of need, but we must depart. I hope we can gain vengeance for your people."

Landor and Joggan embraced. And then that was that! Billy and the bobbits were off once more.

The Swamp of Wiffindor

Billy thought he had been tired before. But he hadn't been. Not really. Not like he was now. He had now reached a level of exhaustion that he had never experienced before. He was so tired that he could have slept standing up. Every single step was a struggle. It felt as if he was walking across a beach of wet sand in a full suit of armour, so heavy were his legs. But, in the last few minutes, Billy had begun to become more alert, because a foul stench had begun to creep into his nostrils and awoken his senses. And the smell seemed to be getting stronger and stronger with every step that they took.

"So, what's the deal with this swamp?" asked Billy. "Why is it so smelly?"

"The swamp is the lowest area of land on our planet," explained Gringo. "Every waterway flows toward, and ends, in the swamp. Each dead fish from every river and any sewage that finds a stream will end up there, where it festers and grows more and more pungent."

"Sewage ends up in the streams?" asked Billy, recalling the countless times he had filled his drinking flask from the rivers during the quest.

"Goblins would happily do their business in the stream. A dwarf filled with fine ales, too." said Gringo, failing to recognise that these facts had made Billy feel quite uneasy. "The stench of the swamp is so terrible that no one has ever succeeded in crossing the bridge that leads across the swamp to the key of Grainter. A few have tried, but the stench is so intense that they have fallen unconscious and end up falling off and drowning in the foul river of pestilence below."

Billy wondered how on Earth he was supposed to do such an impossible task. And then he remembered! A few years ago, Curtis had been on a mountainside picking wildflowers, in the hope that they may prove to have undiscovered medicinal properties, when a bumblebee had flown up his nose, got stuck and stung him. Since then, he could not smell a thing. It was Billy's only pleasure in class; farting, and letting Curtis inhale his stench, without him even noticing!

"So, is there *no* chance at all then that someone with a sense of smell could cross the bridge?" asked Billy nervously.

Joggan shook his head ferociously at the very idea. "No! Anyone foolish enough to try would surely be heading toward certain death. And that is why you must cross the bridge alone, O Great One."

Billy's head began to swim. Was it the stench, or was it panic? The swamp was beginning to really pong now. If Joggan was correct about it leading to certain death, then what was he going to do? He looked at the other bobbits who were now squeezing their noses tightly shut with their fingers to block out the smell.

"Oh, Billy," said Ramsay, "you are so lucky that you cannot smell this foul stench!"

Billy did not respond. It was taking his every effort not to throw up. The stench had seemingly increased tenfold in a truly short space of time. He decided to ask some more questions to try and cistract him for the stink.

"So has the guardian of the key of Grainter got no sense of smell either? He asked. "And how has he survived for so long guarding the key – you said it had been there for thousands of years?"

"Not much is known of the guardian I'm afraid, Sire," said Joggan. "But we do know why they have remained in the swamp for so long. The swamp is *so* stinky that time itself cannot survive at the heart of the swamp. Once the guardian crossed the bridge, they became preserved in the exact same manner as they were on that very day long, long ago!"

Suddenly, Gringo stopped and then so too did the other bobbits.

"This is where we must leave you, Sire," said Gringo, looking like he had just spent a week on a boat in rough tides. "Look, in the far d stance there is the bridge. We shall watch you from here. We cannot go any further. Once you cross the bridge over to the island, the guardian of the key will ask you to speak its name. State the guardian's name and retrieve the key."

Billy's wobbly legs just about carried him towards the bridge. What was he doing? He was walking toward a bridge that would probably lead to his death. And even if he did get across, the guardian would never pass over the vital key - not without Billy knowing the guardian's name. Billy thought about how he could avoid this task, but when he turned back, he saw the bobbits looking on at him with pure hope and admiration and he realised he had only two options - attempt the task or confess! He had come so far that the latter seemed like no option at all. Billy continued to trudge on until finally, he reached the bridge. Even forgetting the smell, crossing the bridge seemed a daunting enough task. The wooden planks on which Billy was to walk on looked older and rottener than a zombie's teeth. And the bridge was strung together by ropes that look so ancient and frayed, it looked like they could be pulled apart by hand.

 Billy took a step onto the bridge. It creaked under his weight. Slowly, he took another step forward and then another and another. All the while Billy had been holding his breath, but eventually the lack of oxygen in his lungs forced him to inhale. And when he did so, the stench smashed him across the face like a heavyweight boxer delivering a knockout blow! Billy's thoughts began to tumble around in his head like a kaleidoscope and the steps beneath him seemed to dance around wildly as his vision blurred and span. Billy felt like fainting, so he grasped his hands tightly on the worn rope and closed his eyes to gather himself.

Suddenly Billy's mind shot back in time to last spring when he went on an overnight camping trip with the school, and he had to share a tent with Gary Barnes. Gary was a pig — the packed lunch his Mum packed him every day was more like a family's picnic basket than a small school time snack. Anyway, during the camping trip the teachers cooked sausages over the fire for the children's supper. After a few minutes, Gary had become impatient, so when the teachers were not looking, he jabbed one with a stick and proceeded to eat it. This was quickly followed by another one being wolfed down. Being all pink and flubbery on the inside, Billy knew that they were not cooked through, but there was no point telling that to greedy Gary. The night that followed was horrific. Billy lay helpless as Gary moaned and wailed and rolled about the tent, burping and farting, as the sausages made their way through his small intestine. The grumbling and bubbling from his stomach made became unbearable for Billy to listen too, for they were always swiftly followed by another jet of foul noxious gas being released into the tent. Billy could remember the smell as clear as day. It was the most odious, putrid smell he would ever smell.

Instantly, Billy opened his eyes and raised his head sharply. If he could spend the night in the tent with Gary Barnes and his belching bottom, then he could do this! Billy inhaled deeply. The smell, while still utterly putrid, did not seem so bad now. Composing himself, Billy took a step forward and then another, and another, and before he knew it, he was halfway across the rickety bridge. Billy remained dizzy and disorientated but continued carefully pacing over the bridge, one step at a time. He felt in control! 'Gary Barne's bum, Gary Barne's bum,' he kept repeating to himself as he continued. And then, just like that, his foot planted on solid ground. He had made it!

Billy looked around. The land before him was completely barren. Not a blade of grass or a chancing weed could be seen from the cracked red-dust ground. Yet, in the distance he could see something. Billy began to walk toward it. His heart began to flutter as he approached, for what was surely the key of Grainter was hanging tantalisingly from a hook upon the end of a metal pole. It was in plain view! As clear as day! Despite being thousands of years old, it looked pristine, sparkling in the sunlight like a precious stone. But one thing puzzled Billy - if this was indeed the key of Grainter, then where was the guardian?

The Guardian

"So, finally, after all these years, someone has come for the key?"

Billy looked around but could not see anyone.

"Down here, you idiot!"

Looking down, Billy noticed a caterpillar sat upon a toadstool. The caterpillar was as black as coal, with a plume of spiky scarlet red feathers running across the length of its tiny back. Crouching down, Billy's eyes met the two small red dots of the caterpillar.

"Are you the guardian of the key of Grainter?" asked Billy, who was unsure because of the creature's tiny stature.

"Do you see anyone else here?" snapped the caterpillar. "And who might you be?"

Billy stood proudly upright and pushing his shoulders back, he declared with great authority, "I am Curtis Hennig, the Chosen One!"

"Well, we'll see about that, won't we?" grumbled the caterpillar. Then the caterpillar just sat staring at Billy. And not in the way that everyone else had looked at him since he arrived. The caterpillar did not look at Billy like he was special - he looked at him in the way that someone looks at a dog poo smeared on the bottom of their shoe. And then the caterpillar spat out the words, "Go on then, if you are the Chosen One, what's my name?" And the caterpillar stared some more.

Billy studied the caterpillar to try and get a sense of what his name could be. He surely could not be something ordinary, like Peter or Paul, so Billy began recalling the names of various species of caterpillars, like cabbage white or red admiral. But this caterpillar was black! Billy could see the caterpillar frowning as it grew impatient.

"Well, come on then, ding-dong head. I am very busy. I haven't got all day," it huffed and puffed.

Billy was at a loss. "Um, Err. Rumplestiltskin?" he blurted out.

"Rumplewhat?" snorted the caterpillar in disgust. "Never heard of him. It certainly isn't me." And shaking his tiny head he said, "You aren't the Chosen One at all. I knew you weren't. You clearly haven't talked to the Tree of Knowledge, and you are certainly not getting the key. Now, be on your way!"

Billy fell to his knees. "No, please!" he pled. "You don't understand. I did go to the Tree of Knowledge, but I wasted my questions." Billy paused for a moment, before continuing. "To be honest, I am not Curtis Hennig. My name is Billy Baggins. The bobbits made a mistake and brought me here instead of him, and now it is up to me to save the world. The evil Lord Mouldywart has many, if not all, of the spirit stones and he is going to destroy the world, unless I stop him. And to do that, I need the key. I need to get the sword of power. There is no other way. Please, I beg you, please give me the key of Grainter."

The caterpillar looked up at Billy. Its tiny mouth broke into a wide grin. "No! You are not having the key. Now, get lost tooba nose!"

Tears welled in Billy's eyes. Was this it? Was this the moment that he finally let down the bobbits? The moment where he failed and let the world be destroyed? Billy looked hopelessly at the key on the hook. It was just sat there in plain view. He was so near, yet so far. The key was just hanging there, like a ripe apple on a tree waiting to be plucked. And then, suddenly, a thought occurred to him.

"So, whatever you name is, are you some sort of great sorcerer? Is that why you were chosen to guard the key?"

"Do I look like a great sorcerer, you idiot?" said the caterpillar, getting ever more irritated. "No one *chose* me to guard the key, I decided to do it myself. I thought it would be a bit of a laugh. Now, why are you still here? I told you to beat it!"

"So," said Billy, "if you are not a sorcerer, what are you?"

"Are you blind as well as stupid, frong face? I'm a caterpillar!"

"Interesting," said Billy, beginning to outstretch his arm. "So, what I'm wondering then is, if you are just a plain and ordinary caterpillar, what you could do to stop me if I wanted to reach up and take the key?"

And then Billy did just that.

"I...I... Get off that key!" raged the caterpillar. At once, the caterpillar's body began swaying up and down, like a wave, as it very-slowly began to move toward Billy.

"Right, don't you move a muscle. I'll be there in a few minutes, and when I do, I'm going to kick your butt!" said the caterpillar, as it inched painfully slowly towards Billy.

Billy looked at the key glistening in his hand. His heart was beating out of his chest. He had it. He had the key of Grainter. "Listen, thanks for all your help,

Rumplestiltskin," he said, "but I'll be off now. I must save the world. You have a nice day."

With that, Billy turned and began walking back towards the bridge.

"Get back here. Are you chicken, boy?" shouted the caterpillar.

Billy ignored it and instead headed back over the bridge. He could hear the faint sound of the caterpillar ranting and raving as he exited and made his way back to the bobbits. He could not wait to show them the key. He knew they would be so happy and so proud. And Billy was happy and proud, too. He had retrieved the key of Grainter. Another major step toward achieving the goal. The quest was nearing completion!

Toward the Misty Mountains

With the key of Grainter in their possession, the final destination was the misty mountains, where Billy was to obtain the sword of power and confront Lord Mouldywart. Billy's initial jubilation of having the key had gradually diminished in the days of trekking towards the mountain that followed. The feeling had, little by little, been replaced by anxiety, fear and trepidation about the final few tasks that lay ahead.

"Only a few more hours and then we shall camp," said Gringo, whose pace always remained steady, no matter how hungry or tired he felt. Hunger was something clearly felt by others in the party, too.

"What's for dinner tonight, Ramsay?" asked Barry.

Billy knew the answer to that question already - frong stew! He had seen Ramsay unearth some of the grubby tubers and put them in his pouch, a few hours ago.

"Frong stew," said Ramsay brightly.

"Mmmmm," said Barry, licking his lips in anticipation.

This would be at least the fifteenth time that Ramsay had cooked frong stew since he arrived. Billy even knew the recipe of by heart himself now. He knew that the frong needed to be boiled hard at first, before reducing the water to a steady simmer after five minutes. This was essential if you wanted to cook it perfectly - so that it is not mushy on the outside, or raw and crunchy in the centre. But even when it was cooked perfectly, it still was a bland and boring vegetable. The last packet of monster munch seemed nothing but a distant memory now. Billy longed for more. There were many things he longed for now. Even things that he didn't ever really care for normally in the human world would now seem a delicacy. And because of this, he had promised himself many times over the course of the quest not to ever take things for granted again. And he felt sure that he would keep to it.

Billy had been with the bobbits for well over a month now. And he could not quite believe that this would only translate to around three hours in Earth time. It would be around four o clock on Sunday morning at home, and Curtis Hennig would probably be tucked up in bed, deep in the middle of his perfect eight-and-a-half-hour sleep, as recommended by doctors.

"Billy, we need to talk about what lies ahead." Joggan had been much quieter over the past few days, seemingly choosing his words carefully, as if he believed them to be limited and was at fear of them running out. Billy sensed that he was getting incredibly nervous about what lay ahead, and this anxiety spread to him, choking him like a creeping weed strangles a plant.

"The sword of power dwells deep in the heart of the misty mountains. Following the traditional route across the mountain range takes days; time we do not have! Fortunately for us, Gringo has scouted a secret tunnel that takes us straight to the sword of power and bypasses unnecessary travelling."

"That's fantastic. Well done, Gringo," said Billy, patting him on the back.

Gringo blushed from head to toe, the bright red of his face only broken by the dark yellow of his proud grin.

"However, this shortcut does come with a downside."

Here we go, thought Billy.

"The tunnel is home to a fearsome troll. Trolls are ghastly creatures and anyone who has the misfortune to encounter one inevitably dies a horrible, gruesome death. Usually by being slowly chewed up and eaten alive. But you, O Chosen One will surely succeed where others have failed. After all, it is written in the prophecy."

And there it was. The reason that Joggan had been so quiet and anxious over the past few days. A fearsome and terrifying troll

And, once again, Billy felt panic rising within him. A feeling he was growing well accustomed to on this quest.

The Troll

A few hours later and the party had reached the entrance to the secret passage through the mountains. And here Billy stood, about to begin another trial that could very easily lead to his untimely death!

"Sire, the prophecy says that the Chosen One will tame the troll with the peaceful strumming of a lute." Joggan smiled. "I believe the lute is not a common instrument in your realm. Thank goodness you can play it with such beauty and ease."

"Yeah, lucky!" said Billy.

"So," said Joggan, "the plan is that you shall enter the cave alone and play the troll a lullaby on the lute and once he drifts off to sleep, you can come out and get us. We will then all creep quietly through the tunnel, straight into the heart of the misty mountains!"

"Yeah, that is one option, but I have another idea," said Billy, desperately seeking another solution. "Why don't we just go the long way through the mountains? Sure, it adds a few days onto the quest, but I am having a great time. You know, all us guys together, chatting, having the banter!"

"I am so glad that you approve of our company, Sire," said Joggan. "But no! There is no time. We do not know how close Lord Mouldywart is to reaching the doorway to the chamber of the Gods. We must take the shortcut!"

"Okay, well then maybe one of you guys could go in before me, just to suss it out for me and get an idea of exactly how big this troll is first? It will give me time to work out which lullaby to play and get my fingers ready," suggested Billy, blowing into cupped hands to pretend to warm them.

The bobbits looked at each other, and then fell about laughing.

"Billy, you are too funny," said Ramsay. "As if we could go in there with that ferocious beast. He would tear our very arms from their sockets. No, Your Excellency, only the Chosen One would dare take on such a ridiculous task."

Billy was trembling like an under-set jelly. What was he to do? He knew that he could not provide the bobbits any good reason why he should not go into the cave. Once again, he would either have to confess or to attempt to serenade the troll. Billy decided that the best plan of action would be to sneak into the cave and check out the situation. Maybe, after he saw what he was dealing with, there would be another way to pass the ogre unseen? Placing his bag down, Billy loosened the drawstring, grasping the neck of the lute and lifting it out of the bag.

"Sire, before you go, would you please play us a song?" asked Gringo.

Billy looked at the strange and foreign object in his grasp. It was useless to Billy. It may as well have been from a Martian spaceship, "Na, I'm saving myself for my big performance!"

"Well Sire," said Barry," if you still need to warm your fingers, you could always give me a Chinese burn, if it will help?" he said, outstretching an arm covered in thick fuzzy fur.

Billy just shook his head.

And then it all went quiet. There was nothing left to say. The only thing left to do was to begin the task. Billy plodded over to the cave entrance and standing sideways to the narrow crack in the rock, squeezed himself through. Once inside, he jiggled in the lute behind him.

Meanwhile Joggan set about lighting a torch. He wrapped a rough scraggly cloth soaked in a flammable ointment around a wooden club with flammable ointment. quickly scraping two stones together provided the spark needed to set it aflame. Joggan passed Billy the lit torch, which he grasped with his spare hand.

And it was only a few steps into the cave when Billy became glad of it. The darkness was unlike anything

Billy had ever experienced before. It felt as dark as death – an uncomfortable thought that would not leave him. He felt terrified. Each time he planted his foot down on the ground it echoed around the cave and Billy was sure it would alert the ogre to his presence. He hesitated at every corner. He carefully peaked around each one to make sure it was safe. After a series of particularly tight twists and turns, Billy noticed a glimmer of light up ahead. As he moved toward it, the tunnel opened into a great cavern. A large opening in the ceiling of the cave cast light into the huge space. A waterfall slowly trickled down the side of the cavern, where it pooled into a great puddle and tricked off in tiny rivers meandering between the rocks.

And then Billy saw something that took his breath away. It was a colossal skeleton! The biggest of the bones were larger and thicker than Billy himself and a tennis court could have sat inside the ribcage. The skull, while smaller in proportion to the rest of the body, was still the size of a van and as Billy gazed upon the he thing with its pronounced jaw and small eye sockets he knew that it was the skeletal frame of an ogre! It had been dead for a good while by the looks of it. Its bones were picked clean of meat and shone a pure white! The relief of this discovery felt to Billy like a cool ocean breeze wafting over him. Released the build-up of fear made Billy feel rather emotional and he could not do anything for a while, but eventually, he turned and scurried back to the entrance of the cave where he called to the bobbits, "Come on guys, it's safe to pass!"

The bobbits quickly scampered over to the mouth of the cave.

"Did you get the troll to sleep, Sire," whispered Joggan, as the bobbits took it in turns to squeeze into the cave, one by one.

"Even better," said Billy. "And you don't need to be so quiet - I killed the troll."

Even in the pitch-black darkness, Billy could still make out the look of amazement and bewilderment upon the faces of the bobbits. "But how did you kill it? "Joggan asked. "I know you are the Chosen One, but no one has ever killed a cave troll before."

"I just did," said Billy. "I didn't want to just put the troll to sleep because he might have woken up when you guys walked past. I did not want to take that risk; if he were to see you, he would have eaten you whole in one bite. You would be like a bobbit nugget to the troll. It was ferocious. I mean, a total beast."

"But your bow was in your rucksack," said Gringo. "How did you defeat it?"

"I just used my hands," said Billy.

The stunned silence of the bobbits was broken when they finally came upon the troll's skeleton because when they did see it, every one of the bobbits gasped so deeply that it is surprising that the torch didn't extinguish from starvation of oxygen.

"But Sire, he is only a Skeleton? I am confused," said Ramsay. "He wouldn't have decayed this quickly?"

Billy half-smiled. "All I can say is that when I go to town on someone, they know about it." He was getting rather carried away with himself. "I just started punching the troll and before I knew it, I had punched all his skin off. And then all its muscles went and then his blood and his organs. Everything!"

"But there is no mess?"

"Well, I punch so hard that everything I hit instantly turns to dust," said Billy, clenching his hands tightly to show the others the power that dwelled in his mighty fists.

"Wow! Do you have any anger left for me?" said Barry, turning his round head to show Billy his supple cheek.

"No, I'm punched out Baz," said Billy, whose cocky and arrogant tone would have been rather grating to anyone other than the boobits. "Come on, let's just plough on, shall we?"

The band of brothers passed by the skeleton and continued through the cave in stunned silence. It was the first time in the whole journey thus far that Gringo had walker slower than normal. He, like all the bobbits, were in utter shock. They had known that the Chosen One was special, but they did not know he was this special!

The Sword of Power

Gringo stopped, held his torch steady and said, "We are here."

If they had reached the sword of power, then it had indeed been a mighty shortcut because they had reached their destination before night had fallen. Not that light and day meant anything in the caves. The flickering torches that Gringo and Joggan had bookended the party with had been just bright enough to lead the way and Billy's eyes had somewhat adjusted to the darkness. But it was still very dark, and awfully hard to see.

Gringo began waving his torch around to illuminate the room they found themselves in and every now and again the dancing flames licked an edge of steel. Billy knew at once that this was the sword of destiny and he jostled and fidgeted through the bobbits to get a better view. But he need not have bothered.

Gringo held his torch against the side of the wall and kept it steady.

Instantly a brilliant flash of green flame exploded into existence. And then another next to it. And then several more. Billy continued to enjoy the dazzling firework display before him, and when it finally ceased, a long stream of luminous green lights flickered around the whole edge of the room, illuminating it a beautiful emerald hue.

And now it was clear as day. In the centre of the room was a broad sword with an intricate golden handle, adorned with delicate sparkling jewels. The very tip of the sword was hidden in a block of smooth polished stone. And at the far end of the room was a tunnel, now also illuminated in bright green lights, winding off into who knows where.

"There it is," said Joggan "The sword of power!"

The bobbits then parted, Joggan and Barry to the left and Ramsay and Gringo to the right, leaving a clear pathway for Billy to walk through.

"Billy, go forth and pull the sword from the stone," said Joggan.

Slowly, Billy paced up to the sword in the stone. His every footstep echoed lonelily around the great cavern. The bobbits were statues. You could have cut the tension with a knife.

As Billy approached the sword, he glanced over around at his bobbit companions. They all looked so proud, so amazed an in awe of the prophecy being fulfilled. Joggan even had tears welling in his eyes.

Billy placed his sweaty palms around the handle and squeezed his hands tightly together. He took a deep breath to summon every ounce of strength he had within him, and he pulled. He pulled with all his might. He yanked that sword like a demonic dentist pulling a hesitant tooth. Beads of sweat gathering on his brow and his face turned crimson with effort. Billy strained so hard he thought he might explode. He willed the sword to move from its stone with every fibre of his being.

He needed it to move.

It must move.

But it did not move!

Finally, when he could pull no more, Billy released his grip.

Billy looked at the bobbits and the bobbits looked at Billy. The look of awe in their eyes had been replaced by confusion.

No one knew what to say but someone had to say something, so Barry said, "Come on Billy, try again. You can do it!"

Billy gazed upon the sword. Barry was right, he could do this. It was only the very tip of the sword that was encased in stone. One mighty tug would surely release it if he really believed. Once again, Billy grabbed the handle. He anchored his feet to the floor and with every muscle in his body he began to pull.

Barry made his way up to Billy and began to chant his name for encouragement.

"Billy, Billy, Billy."

Billy continued to pull, but the sword was not loosening.

"Billy. Billy. Billy."

Billy's sweaty palms were slipping and sliding off the handle, as if he were trying to hold onto a wriggling fish.

"Billy, Billy, Billy."

Billy did not have much left to give.

"Billy, Billy, Billy."

"SHUT UP!"

Billy released his grasp from the sword and flung his arm backwards. The back of his hand clattered into Barry's face with a terrible thud, knocking him to the floor.

"Oh my!" cried Barry. "What a wonderous day. The hand of the Chosen One has kissed my face. This is truly a blessing."

But Billy just dashed out of the room with tears in his eyes. What had he done?

The Chosen One or Chosen Wrong?

Billy sat at the edge of the dark cave tunnel, buried his head into his arms and began to sob. What had he done to poor Barry? Worse still, he had let everyone down. So far, he had kept up the act of being the Chosen One so well. He had saved the bobbits from a hungry wolf, rescued Joggan from a gang of goblins and despite wasting his three wishes at the Tree of Knowledge, he had managed to cross the bridge at the swamp of Wiffendor and retrieve the sacred key of Grainter. But now he had fallen at the final hurdle. The sword would not release from the stone so he would not be able to destroy Lord Moldywart and the bobbits and everything in their world would perish. If only he had told the truth from the beginning, the bobbits would have been able to get Curtis and then the real Chosen One would have been able to save the world! But as Billy sat there feeling sorry for himself, Joggan approached.

"Sire, may I have a word?" he said, placing a reassuring furry hand on his back.

"Is Barry alright?" Billy asked.

"Barry is fine," replied Joggan. "More than fine - he is delighted. He will not stop talking about it. There will be a fine bruise in the morning. That will thrill him even more."

It did not make Billy feel any better

"I feel terrible," said Billy. "I never meant to hurt him."

Joggan nodded his head in understanding, paused and said, "Sire, I am confused what happened in there? Why did you not pull the sword from the stone?"

Once again, Billy burst into a flood of tears. He sobbed like he had never done before. Weeks of tiredness and stress and anxiety poured out of him, escaping in the form of tears from his eyes. "I'm sorry, Joggan. I tried, I really did, but it wouldn't budge." Billy wiped the wetness from his face. "Look, I think it's time to come clean." And then he paused. He really did not want to say what he was about to say - but he had to! "I'm so sorry but I am not the Chosen One. I am not Curtis Hennig, I am Billy Baggins. And I don't live at number 36 Wessington Avenue, I live at number 39 - three doors down. You made a mistake, and I just didn't tell you. I am not special like Curtis is. I am not special at all. I'm a nobody. I have got no skills, no talents. Nothing!"

Joggan just smiled at Billy as if he had not heard a single word that had come out of his mouth.

"All of these things you say are things we already know," he said.

"What do you mean? You knew I am not Curtis Hennig? When did you find out? Why did you not say? Why aren't you cross? Why...why?"

None of this made any sense to Billy.

"We knew from the start. It was no mistake that we came to your house, *39* Wessington Avenue. We knew you were Billy Baggins and not Curtis Hennig. You see there is something written in the prophecy that you do not know. It states that you, Billy Baggins, are the

Chosen One and you will leac us to victory in the great war, but you will only accomplish this task by pushing yourself to prove yourself more able than this Curtis Hennig."

Billy shook his head. "But all the tasks were perfect for Curtis. Like talking with the animals and firing a bow and the fact Curtis has no sense of smell. It is like all the challenges were all designed especially for him."

"And yet, you completed them all. The prophecy does not say the Chosen One is an expert archer, only that he will save a bobbit with a bow. It does not state the Chosen one has no sense of smell, only that he will cross the bridge and retrieve the key of Grainter. It doesn't say the Chosen one will soothe the ogre with a lute, it just stays the Chosen One will lead the bobbits through a tunnel guarded by an ogre."

Then Joggan looked at Billy. He really looked at him, as if he were looking through his body and speaking to his soul.

"And the prophecy also says that Billy Baggins — the Chosen One - will retrieve the sword of destiny and defeat Lord Mouldywart!"

"But I can't pull up the sword. You saw; it didn't move!"

"Billy, try again."

"Why? It's hopeless."

"Please, Billy. Try again - you just need to believe."

Billy felt like his head had just gone twelve rounds with a heavyweight boxer. He did not know what to think any more.

"Alright, I'll give it one more go."

Joggan outstretched his arm. Billy took a firm grasp of his hand and Joggan pulled him to his feet. And then the pair walked in tandem back into the cavern that housed the sword of power. As they entered, Billy could hear Barry's excited ramblings. "The best way I can describe it is that it felt like a sturdy hammer hitting a nail square on its head. It was glorious. I felt each one of his strong knuckles as they collided into my….

Barry immediately stopped talking when he became aware that Billy had entered.

Billy could not bring himself to look at Barry after what he had done, so he walked straight past the bobbits and over the sword in the stone. Once again, he placed his hand around the handle. He took in a deep breath and held it. At least it would be all over in a few minutes. If he could not do it then at least he could go home. Billy clenched his hands tght, and he pulled. Suddenly, Billy flew backwards, because the sword had shot out of the stone as if it were a knife sat in block of warm butter. Billy had not even felt it come out of the stone. Billy picked himself up from the floor, before thrusting the sword proudly into the air.

As the sword went up the bobbits went down, lowering themselves down on bended knees and bowing their heads solemnly. Slowly, Joggan raised his head. "Billy, you are now if the possession of the sword of power. You truly are the Chosen One. Now, let us finish this, once and for all!"

Lord Mouldywart Awaits!

The gang kept pace with Gringo as he hastily scurried through the tunnel at the far end of the room. When they reached the entrance, it was obvious that the tunnel was extremely long. The green lights at the sides of the wall seem to stretch on forever into the distance, so there was no telling how long it was. But they needed to take the tunnel, so take the tunnel they did. After a few minutes, the party could no longer see the room that hosed the sword of power anymore. They pressed on.

They had been walking for around ten minutes now.

The sword of power felt heavy in Billy hands, which made it feel like much longer. But just as the tunnel felt like it would never end, suddenly, it did and Billy and the bobbits found themselves an enormous room. The room was far, far bigger than the one that held the sword of power. The green lanterns that Gringo has set in motion lined this room, too. And there, set into one of the vast walls, stood a colossal door, at least thirty feet high. The orange to deep brown bronze gates were beautifully decorated with images of the seven Gods and Goddesses as well as many creatures that Billy had encountered on his travels.

They rushed over to the door. Billy ran his hand over the door but felt no seal. There was no handle with which to open it. No way in which to enter. But then Billy noticed that around the door were seven holes, presumably for where the sacred stones were to be set, and he intuitively knew that the stones were the key. The party then spent several minutes examining the beautifully decorated door in wonder, until Billy reached a point where he felt he could close his eyes and recall every detail.

"It is magnificent," said Ramsay.

"More wonderous the prophecy describes," added Joggan.

"Beautiful," said Gringo, before changing the subject. "I am surprised we arrived here before the elves. Our shortcut must have hastened our journey more than I anticipated. But they surely cannot be far behind."

"So, what do we do now?" Billy asked.

"Now we have nothing to do but wait," Joggan replied. "We wait for our eleven allies, anc we wait until Lord Mouldywart arrives to attempt to open the door. And when he does, we will begin a great battle and you will destroy him with your sword of power."

Billy sat down. But then he stood back up again. He did not know what to do with himself. He had ants in his pants. They had finally reached the final destination of the epic quest and Billy could not wait a moment longer to finish all this and return home. "How long do you think we'll be waiting?" he asked.

"It could be minutes, it could be days, weeks. It could be months!"

"Months? I cannot wait here for months." Billy said.

"Fear not, Sire," said Gringo. "We had anticipated this, so we all spent much time before your arrival preparing some festivities to entertain us while we wait. Joggan has numerous stories about our land, Ramsey is going to go through his favourite recipes and Barry has some poetry that he has written."

Barry was bubbling with excitement, bobbing up and down like a rowboat on a stormy sea.

"And I have many a joke from my court jester days," said Gringo. "So, I shall begin proceedings." He stopped and smiled as if he was telling himself the joke in his head before uttering it and he was finding it rather amusing. "What do you call a bobbit who had gone many moons without a granush?"

The bobbits all looked at each other, shrugging their shoulders and shaking their heads.

"We do not know?" said Ramsay.

After a brief hush, Gringo responded. "An empty cocoffin!"

Throwing their heads back and breaking into a fit of laughter, the bobbits held their bellies as if the laughter were going to explode out of them if they did not psychically hold it in. ⌐his went on for several minutes, until eventually the titters died down.

"I guess you have to be a bobbit to get that one," said Billy. He knew that this could be a long wait.

Why are we Waiting?

Had it been months? It felt like it. Gringo had exhausted his joke book and Ramsay was onto the final recipe from his book.

"And then you mix into the gringus root and cook until reduced by half. Then serve with grated frong."

"Brilliant," said Joggan. "Who knew that listening to hundreds of recipes would be so interesting?"

And now it was Barry's turn. It was clear to see that Barry was nervous. He had worked hard on his poetry at various junctures of the quest. After mealtimes especially was when inspiration seemed to catch him, and he would often be seen scribbling thoughts and ideas into the small notebook he held in his rucksack. Barry held this notebook in his slightly wobbly hands. He coughed a little to clear his throat, before beginning.

"My face is really round and big.

My face looks like a lovely pig.

I really love the Chosen One,

I love his hair and I love his thumbs."

A moment of silence was observed, before the bobbits erupted into a round of thunderous applause.

"Fantastic, Barry," said Ramsay, eyes moist with tears. "That stirred emotions deep within me."

Barry looked at Billy with doe eyes. "Did you like it, Sire?" he asked timidly, a hopeful look hanging on his face.

"It was absolutely brilliant," said Billy. "Truly astonishing. Easily the best poem I have ever heard." Stroking Barry's ego helped ease his guilt over hitting him earlier.

"So, you would like to hear more?" asked Barry.

Billy was just about to say that he needed to preserve his energy, when suddenly, a faint beating sound began to drift into the earshot. The beating got louder and louder - it was the sound of an army of drums!

"Joggan stood up. "This is it, comrades. This is surely Lord Mouldywart and his army of cave dwellers!" Billy and the remaining bobbits quickly sprang to their feet. And then they just stood quietly, trying to make out how many drums there were. How big was the army? Billy found it hard to tell, because he was not sure what was beating louder – the drums or his heart. But that there was a lot! The drumming continued to get louder and stronger. And so, did Billy's heartbeat.

And then suddenly, the pounding ceased. The party stood watching the entrance of the cavern.

And then a dark figure glided into the room. It appeared that its feet hovered a few inches from the ground. The creature wore a long, black cloak and straggly black hair covered its face like a dirty veil, making it hard to tell what it looked like. The creature's clawed hand clutched a thick wooden staff.

"Are you, Lord Mouldywart?" Billy asked, his voice sounding exceedingly small in such a large room.

The creature raised his head. And as he did, the gang now got a good look at the creature. He did look like an elf, but like an elf gone goth. His hair was not the pure white that Billy had seen on the other elves, it was black as death. He had a tattoo on his cheek, that looked perhaps like a dragon, but it was hard to tell for sure as the tattoo was terrible! It was as if Lord Mouldywart had fallen asleep on a puddle of wet ink and woken up to find it had stained his face. It was far easier to make out the colour of his eyes, for they were a brilliant blue and they glistened in the darkness, like sapphires. Rings of various sizes and thicknesses were punched through his nose and ears and eyebrows and across his shoulder was a napsack, filled with something – the seven sacred stones!

"Yes, I am he," said the creature, whose voice was far higher and squeakier than a powerful evil sorcerer's should be.

"And who may you be?" asked Lord Mouldywart, despite clearly knowing.

"I am the Chosen One. I am the one who is going to stop you from entering the chamber of the Gods." said

Billy, believing it a little more than he did a few hours ago, but certainly still not for sure.

Lord Mouldywart looked Billy up and down. "You? The Chosen One? You are nothing but a small and pathetic child. I have no fear of you. I could crush you and your friends like ants. Tiny helpless ants. And unless you move out of my way right now, then that is exactly what I shall do!"

Was Lord Mouldywart right? Even after everything he had been through and what he had been told by Jogggan, Billy still harboured serious doubts that he was the Chosen One and further doubted whether he could defeat this powerful dark wizard before him. But, throughout the quest, he had become exceptionally good at hiding his doubts.

"Look, if you give us the stones and return to the caves then we can forget about this. There doesn't need to be bloodshed here today."

Lord Mouldywart threw his head back and laughed a crackling, sinister laugh. "Sorry, I was just thinking

142

about what happened earlier. One of my cave dwellers fell over of a slippery patch and hurt his bottom." And then he suddenly stopped laughing and went profoundly serious. "But no, I will not give you the stones. I think that instead, I shall use them to enter the chamber of the Gods and rule this land once and for all. But before I do that, I think I will kill you!"

With that, Lord Mouldwart thrust his staff outward. A halo of white electricity began to crackle and dance around the tip of the staff before it became so full of bristling energy that it could not be contained and it shot off the end, sending a blazing ball of light toward Billy. It flew at such a pace that Billy did well to dive out of the way in time. The ball then crashed into the wall, loosening the rocks and sending a shower of pebbles to the floor.

Billy jumped back up onto his feet.

"Use your sword, Billy," called out Joggan. "It will repel his fireballs. Try and get close to him and slay him, ending this once and for all!"

Billy readied his sword.

At that moment, a band of strange looking creatures burst into the room.

The cave dwellers had very pale skin, almost translucent, and were hunched over like old fogies with bad backs. They were painfully thin – every bone in their bodies could clearly be seen underneath the paper-thin skin. Their eyes were huge and dark saucers.

"Kill him, said Lord Mouldywart, pointing squarely at Billy.

Instantly, the cave dwellers charged awkwardly at Billy. There were hundreds of them. Thousand maybe. And they poured into the cave like raging water. Some had daggers, some had catapults, some clubs of wood. All had burning hatred in their big black eyes.

Joggan pulled his slender sword from its sheath. "I will protect you, Sire!" he roared over the sound of the oncoming stampede. "Just make sure that Lord

Mouldywart does not fix the scared stones into the door."

Joggan then began charging toward the cave dwellers, who were charging right at him and within seconds the two collided with a clink of metal as their swords met.

Joggan was nimble in combat. His arms were moving up and down, to the left to the right at such speed it was hard to even see them. He slayed many cave dwellers in a short space of time, but there were too many of them to keep it up. There were at least a hundred cave dwellers surrounding Joggan now and he was but one bobbit. And as the cave dwellers swarmed on top of him it became impossible to see Joggan any longer.

But Gringo was also a brave bobbit. Upon seeing his friend in danger, he pulled a long dagger sharply from its casing in his sock and began to charge at the rabble of cave dwellers. And then he too, was consumed by the pale smoke.

Ramsay was less useful - about as useful as a chocolate teapot in fact, but he too showed courage. Pulling a wooden ladle from his backpack, he stormed toward the cave dwellers, yelling a recipe at the top of his voice.

"One cup of graneek, two ounces of bloory!"

Ramsay stood at the edge of the melee and began beating one of the cave dwellers on the top of its head with the spoon.

It was not enough. Pockets of cave dwellers had managed to burst free and had begun a charge toward Billy. Barry, who had stood still motionless so far, had seen enough.

"I must protect the Chosen One!" he said.

With that, he bent over and hurtled toward the cave dwellers, dispatching them with his very own powerful weapon - his head. Swishing and swashing his melon ball back and forth as he ran, Barry swatted away the cave dwellers like flies. Barry had now bashed about ten cave dwellers. As another half-dozen approached, he once again smashed them away, sending them colliding into the wall with a tremendous thud. As the cave dwellers lay winded and unconscious on the ground Barry continued to hurtle on, right into the heart of huge battle that was occurring in the middle of the room. Barry continued to jerk his head around and as he did so, cave dwellers began flying through the air, like shuttlecocks being swatted away by a racket. Sometimes it seems that courage and determination are more powerful than weapons and fine armoury.

All this had thinned out the cave dwellers a bit and Gringo and Joggan once again came into view. The bobbits now had more room to wield their weapons and fend of the cave dwellers. But there were still far too many of them and with Joggan, Gringo, Ramsay and Barry tiring, this was a battle the bobbits surely could not win.

Parroooo! Parroooo!

Two bursts of a great horn heralded the arrival of the elves. The graceful pixie-like creatures streamed into the cave and crazy dance of swords and weapons ensued. It was manic. Far too calamitous to see exactly what was happening, but Billy believed his team to be winning because he saw many limbs of the cave dwellers being thrown into the air with accompanying jets of crimson blood as they were chopped off. It was disgusting really, like a liquidiser full of ripe tomatoes being turned on without a lid. The battle continued. It was frantic, it was chaotic, it was crazy, it was wild. But then, all-of-a-sudden, a volcanic roar erupted from the centre of it all.

"Halt!"

And that is exactly what happened. Everything stopped. And then, from the middle of the whole thing a familiar voice arose, "I am bursting for a wee." It was Gringo and his small bobbit bladder. "Does anyone else need a wee?" he asked, seeming a little bit embarrassed that he had to stop this important battle to relive himself.

But a hand went up. Then another. Then three more, and before long nearly half of the room had their hands raised. "Are you sure now that this is everyone? Asked Gringo "We are not going to stop again."

"Wait!" rasped the metallic voice of a cave dweller. "I wish for a wee too, but I couldn't raise me hand. Both of me arms have been chopped off!"

"Right, we go for a wee and resume in three minutes," said Gringo. "The bad guys this side, elves and bobbits this side. Just as the two parties were about to split, a cave dweller croaked up, "My friend says that he needs a poo. Is he allowed?"

By this stage Lord Mouldywart had seen and heard enough. "This is absurd!" he bellowed, casting his eye across the sea of creatures before him. "There are to be no poos! We have no time for that. You may have a poo when I am seated in the chamber of the Gods. Until then, you must hold it in." He folded his arms and frowned to show his deep dis-satisfaction about how this was all unfolding.

Hastily, the cave dwellers scuttled over to one side of the room and the bobbits and elves the other. Streams of amber liquid trickled down the walls, forming bronze puddles in the grooves of the bumpy stone floor. Eventually everyone finished up and turned again to face each other. Because he had stopped it, Gringo decided he needed to start it again, "Ready, steady, go!"

And once more the battle commenced, as if it had never stopped.

The only two not engaged in battle were Billy and Lord Mouldywart.

"It doesn't need to be this way, boy," he cackled. "I can send you home now. You could be back in the warmth and comfort of your bed in the blink of an eye." Lord Mouldywart held up a glowing orb. "You don't want to die here. This is not your world. It is not your battle. Just step into the portal and return home."

Billy did not even think about it.

"Never!" he said.

"Very well," said Lord Mouldywart. He then shook his wooden staff from side to side to build up the energy at the end and, as before, a great fireball crackled and whizzed towards Billy, pulsating with a furious energy. Billy threw himself out of the way just in time.

Billy stood. Lord Moldywart was about to send another ball his way when Billy remembered what Joggan had told him. Billy raised the sword of power. It felt heavy and cumbersome in his small hands. But as the oncoming electric ball approached, he managed to muster the power to swing the sword and the tip of it chopped the ball of energy and it exploded with a tremendous bang, showering the ground with sparkles of brilliant white light.

Lord Mouldywart was angered by this. Immediately he shot another missile from the end his wooden staff.

And then another and another. But the sword no longer felt heavy in Billy's hands. It was as if the jolt of the last fireball had awoken it and now yielding and swinging the sword was effortless. The sword seemed to be alive and completely in tune with Billy's thoughts. Wherever Billy wanted the sword to go it would follow. More and more and more energy balls flew at him, but Billy and his sword danced a merry waltz. Billy led with confidence and the sword kept perfectly in time. Billy only had to think it, and the sword would do it.

With every flick of his wrist, a pure white fireball shot from Lord Mouldywart's staff. And each time Billy swatted it away with ease. He felt at one with his weapon. It was as if his arms were working independently from his body as he twisted and turned the sword to meet every oncoming fireball. It had become effortless.

Billy now had the measure of Lord Mouldywart's fireballs, and it also appeared that the bobbits and elves were overcoming the cave dwellers.

Suddenly, Lord Moldywart stopped. He scanned the room and a wicked smile crept deliciously across his lips. Lord Moudywart focused his gaze upon the crowd, before sending another laser ball from his staff. This one flew towards Barry and when it struck him, it sent Barry shooting across the cavern as if he been hit by a speeding train. Barry smashed into the cave wall with an enormous bang, falling to the floor in an untidy heap.

Billy turned back to face Lord Mouldywart. Anger burned in his eyes. "No one hurts my Barry," he screamed as he began to charge toward Lord Mouldywart. Lord Mouuldwart held his staff tightly in his long bony fingers. A swirl of light grew larger upon the end of his staff. And then the whole staff began to shake wildly as if the light was desperate to free itself. Lord Mouldywart readied himself to fire one final extraordinarily large and powerful energy bolt at his foe.

Meanwhile, by now most of the cave dwellers lay slain on the floor and as the elves took care of the last few troublesome creatures, Gringo managed to free himself from battle and call over to Billy.

"Billy, look," he said. Billy briefly took his eyes of Lord Mouldywart and followed Gringo's finger up to the ceiling of the cavern where a large piece of rock hung precariously over Lord Mouldywart, like a root from a child's tooth clinging onto its gummy life raft.

And then Lord Mouldywart released the thunderbolt from his staff. It flew at such a speed that most would not have even seen it coming. But everything had slowed down for Billy. It was like time had stood still and so it was no problem for him to bat the ball of energy upwards, up to the roof of the cavern. The force of the great energy ball was easily enough to break the great rock free, and it dropped down straight and true, landing directly on top of Lord

Mouldywart. No one moved a muscle. No one could quite believe it. Gringo, Joggan and Ramsay dashed over and inspected the rock and what lay beneath. All that could be seen from underneath was pair of ankles covered in black and white striped socks and a fancy shoe of ruby red boots.

But every other part of Lord Mouldywart was squelched. Smashed and smished to smithereens underneath colossal stone.

Lord Mouldywart was dead!

Billy had saved the world!

The End

The battle was over. The war was won. The remaining few cave dwellers, without leadership, had little interest in fighting and fled back through the tunnels to lead the lives they once lived. The elves and bobbits had been victorious. And it had been a great victory. Some elves of course had been injured in battle but not many. It was clear that the cave dwellers were not a fighting folk. There many numbers had proven their only advantage. It had been men against boys.

By now the elves had realised that it was all over and were already celebrating. A little at first but the noise had become ever louder and more joyous as it all sunk in.

Billy though had no desire for celebration. Racing over to Barry, who still lay motionless on the stone floor, he cradled his head in his arms. "Barry, are you okay? Wake up, Barry!"

But Barry did not wake up.

"Barry, please," said Billy. And great tears began to well in his eyes. Great big tears that were too big to his eyes to hold.

Spit, spot. No, it was not Mary Poppins entering the cave to deliver a spoonful of sugar to the injured folk, it was the sound of Billy's tears dripping on Barry's face. By now the other bobbits had gathered round, they too deeply worried for the safety of their comrade.

"Is he dead?" asked Billy.

No bobbit seemed to know.

More tears fell onto Barry's face.

"what...happened?" rose a weary voice.

Billy looked down.

Barry was opening his eyes!

"Barry are you okay?" Billy asked, shaking Barry in his excitement, completely forgetting that he had just suffered major head injury.

"I.....believe so? What happened?"

"What happened?" said Billy. "You saved us is what happened."

Barry was beginning to come around. He groggily got to his feet, before asking in a puzzled tone, "I saved the day?"

"Yes, said Billy, who felt as excited as he had ever felt in his whole life. When your head hit the wall, you loosened a great rock - the rock which squashed Lord Mouldywart flat!"

Barry seemed completely unsure what to do with this information.

"Barry, did you hear me? You saved the day. You are a hero."

"I am?" asked Barry, still confused. Fragments of thoughts then began piecing together in his mind, like a puzzle "If I did indeed save the day, then may I ask something of you, Sire?"

"Anything," said Billy.

"Will you hit me with your beloved fists - one more time?"

Barry closed his eyes and smi ed in anticipation.

"I can go one better than that," said Billy, throwing his arms around Barry's neck and giving him the cuddle of his life. Billy didn't care now. Heck, he even gave Barry a slobbery kiss on the cheek.

"Oh, my!" said Barry. "I cannot describe how happy I am in this moment, your Excellency. I am touched beyond words."

And the feeling of happiness spread through the cave and was palpable in everyone within it.

"So, what now?" asked Billy

"There is one more thing we must do," said Joggan. "We must retrieve the stones from Lord Mouldywart. We cannot leave them here."

Everyone looked at each other, no-one really wanted to do that. How would they do that?

"Those stones must be placed in a scared place – we cannot leave them here."

It took the party several hours to remove the huge boulder from Lord Mouldywart. The elves had to return the forest and bring back huge sticks with which to lever it off him. It took a lot of elf power to complete the job. And when the boulder finally came off it was not a pretty sight! The squashed corpse of Lord Mouldywart was so vile that it cannot be described in detail in this book, for it was, you would have terrible nightmares for many a year.

But despite Lord Moudywart being as flat as a pancake, when the party took the scared stones from his knapsack, they remained pristine, with not a scratch upon them. And they were beautiful. Seven hunks of smooth rock, all glistening a different sparkiling clear and wonderous colour.

"So, what will we do with these stones now," said Billy as they all stood around them gazing.

"It is amazing to think that we could enter the realm of the Gods if we wished," said Joggan. "But that would be a wildly dangerous and irresponsible thing, so this is what I suggest."

Joggan went on to explain that the bobbits would hide three of the stones in secure locations across the realm and the elves would conceal another three. But to prevent such an event like this from ever happening again, the final stone was to be kept in a secure location in a far, far away land.

"Are you happy to take the stone back to your realm?" Joggan asked Billy. "Will you keep it safe and secure?"

"I will," said Billy, feeling every inch the Chosen One now.

Bending down, Billy picked up the stone-coloured yellow. Landor took the blue and red and orange stones and Joggan the green and purple and pink.

And then the parties then said their farewells. It was an odd thing. After what had happened today, saying goodbye and going back to normality seemed a very strange and lien idea. But that was what was needed.

And then, when all was done, they all began their journey home.

Back in the Village

It took a week to arrive back at the bobbit village, walking as the crows fly. Without stopping to slay this thing, or gather that thing, helped. And when Billy and the bobbits strode into their homely village they were ten feet taller than when they had left. It was only minutes after their return that the entire village swarmed from their houses and crowded the streets, like ants escaping an under-threat nest. And it was sheer pandemonium. Bobbits cried, screamed, jumping around and embraced. No one knew what to do with the sheer amount of joy they had within them! Among this chaos, Billy found a pocket of space and he headed over to that hut he had arrived in all that time ago. He entered, and sat on a thick, wooden bench. It was nice to be by himself. Weeks of chaos and noise and danger had drained him completely. He just sat, happy to be enjoying a bit of peace. But he did not have long to enjoy the silence.

Potrab entered the room. He did not speak; he just walked up to Billy and threw his wide arms around him. The familiar smell of cabbage came back. The others must have seen Billy enter the room too for they began to follow in drips and drabs. First Joggan, then Gringo and Ramsay together and finally, Barry.

"Billy, what you have done for us is beyond words," said Potrab. "You did not need to come here. A lesser human would have ignored our pleas. But not you. You stood tall and faced every danger, for our people. You have saved our planet and every living thig in it, and it is something that no-one will ever forget. The prophecy is now legend. You are truly, the Chosen One."

Potrab walked over to the great doors that opened into the village.

"Now, let us feast!"

Potrab placed his hand on the door when Billy stopped him in his tracks.

"No. Stop. Wait!" he said.

Potrab turned around.

"I would love another feast. I would love to join you all and celebrate, but I think it is time for me to go home. I want to get back to my world, I want to get home to my Mum."

This had been somewhat expected by Potrab, because no sooner had Billy uttered these words when Potrab reached into his pocket and taken out the final orb.

"As the Chosen One wishes." he said.

The happiness in the room had flipped into sadness in a very short space of time. After everything that had happened, after the trials, tribulations and friendship that had grown over the journey, Billy did not know how to say goodbye. Nor did the bobbits.

"We shall miss you, Billy," said Ramsay, "What you have done for us is amazing."

"No, thank you" said Billy, giving Ramsay a firm shake of his hand. "Your food is what gave me the strength to achieve those tasks. And everything you made was delicious."

Ramsay smiled.

"Billy, you are an inspiration to all of us," said Gringo, tears filling his eyes.

"I shall miss you, Gringo," said Billy. "You were so helpful to me, I couldn't have done it without you."

"Sire, to be a part of all this was the greatest honour that could ever have fallen upon me," said Joggan, staring intently at Billy. "I know you saved the world, but I shall also never forget the kindness and bravery you showed in saving my life," he said.

"You would have done the same for me. What you have done for me, Joggan, is beyond words," said Billy. "You are a true friend – as are you, Barry," said Billy, beckoning him over.

"I...don't want you to go," said Barry, with a look of true melancholy on his face. "Do you have to go?" he said, choking back tears.

"I do," said Billy. "But I will always remember you, Barry. You were the most helpful bobbit of all. You are a true friend."

And then Billy and all the bobbits came together in a big group embrace. No one knew who was hugging who, but it did not matter, the sense of friendship radiated from everyone.

Eventually, the embrace softened and then ceased.

"I think it's time," said Billy. Potrab said nothing. He just releasing the orb that shattered into a million pieces on the floor, releasing the powerful lightrise within in

Billy looked one last time at each of the bobbits, before stepping into it.

"I'll miss you guys," he said.

"We shall miss you more," said Ramsay.

"You never know, we may even meet again one day in the future," said Gringo.

"But whatever happens, we shall always be in your heart and you in ours," said Joggan.

"And whenever you kick a ball, or see a full moon or a big plate, or anything big and round really, promise me you will think of me, said Barry.

"I will," promised Billy.

And then the lightrise became ever-so bright. Billy closed his eyes and felt that tight squeeze once again until Billy felt that he wasn't in the bobbit village anymore and that he was somewhere else entirely.

Back Home

Wearily, Billy opened his sticky eyes. What time was it? It felt like the middle of the night, but then why was the room so bright. Stretching open his eyes Billy focused his eyes and what he saw - was familiar.

"Morning, Love," said Mum, pulling open the curtains and letting the raging light shine in. "You're having a great lie in, aren't you? You would swear you have been up half the night."

If only she knew!

Billy's Mum walked over and sat her ample bottom down at the bottom of the bed. "Listen, I want to apologise about yesterday," she said. "I was only tired is all. I didn't mean to shout."

Billy smiled. "That's okay, Mum," he said "I know that I could do more around the house. I promise – *I really promise* - that I will help more from now on. If you want, I will clean the floors today to get rid of all the muck I brought in and I can hoover up and I can…

"There's no need for all that," said Mum, shaking her head. "You are only a child, the only thing you need to worry about is enjoying yourself." She stood up from the bed. "I was thinking today I could take you out to the cinema, there's that new Narnia film out, and then you can have whatever you like for tea, you can even have a whole multi-packet of monster munch, if that's what you want?"

"Actually, I was thinking of cooking for you tonight, Mum. I looked up a great recipe for frong, I mean, potato stew."

Mum shook her head in disbelief. "What happened to you during the night? You seem to have gone to bed one boy and woken up another. But don't forget that I love the Billy Baggins that was always here."

Billy smiled. Mum smiled back.

"I am sorry again about yesterday, darling," said Mum. "I didn't mean to compare you to Curtis. I know you don't like that. And I hope you know that I would never swap you for him. Not in a million years.

Between you and me, Cynthia's having terrible trouble with him at the minute. He does not want to go to that posh school. He has been crying about it all the time, saying that he will get homesick. Cynthia says he cries if he is ever without her for more than an hour. It's called attachment disorder," she said, clearly thinking she was awfully intelligent for knowing such a thing. "For all his skills and talent, he's actually a bit of a wet lettuce."

And she quickly popped her hand over her mouth as if she knew she should not have said such a thing.

"Ah, he's okay really," said Billy. "If it will help, I can go over and have a chat with him about it, if you and Cynthia want."

Mum was flabbergasted. "I really do not know what has got into you," she said, looking Billy up and down as if to check he was still her son. "Right, get changed and we'll head off to the shops. You can buy the ingredients you need for this potato stew, and we can get some monster munch."

And then Mum left the room, looking back and smiling again at Billy, before closing the door behind her.

Billy jumped out of bed. He sniffed at the armpits of his top that lay crumpled on the floor, before throwing it over his head. Then he yanked his jeans up to his waist, fiddled with his waistband and crammed his feet into his dirty shoes, twisting them around until his heels fell into place.

Then he placed the sacred yellow stone into the second drawer of his chest of drawers, covering it with pants and socks. He would have to think of a better hiding place for the stone, in time.

He closed the drawer and smiled to himself. What an adventure he had had, I guess extraordinary things do happen to ordinary boys living ordinary lives.

Billy left the room, flicked off the light switch and went downstairs.

And the wardrobe sat in the corner of the room, content in the knowledge that it too had played a part.